SAVING Sky

DIANE STANLEY

HARPER
An Imprint of HarperCollinsPublishers

Novels by Diane Stanley

Bella at Midnight
The Mysterious Case of the Allbright Academy
The Mysterious Matter of I. M. Fine
A Time Apart

Saving Sky

Copyright © 2010 by Diane Stanley

All rights reserved. Printed in the United States of America.

No part of this book may be used or reproduced in any manner whatsoever without written permission except in the case of brief quotations embodied in critical articles and reviews. For information address HarperCollins Children's Books, a division of HarperCollins Publishers, 10 East 53rd Street, New York, NY 10022.

www.harpercollinschildrens.com

Library of Congress Cataloging-in-Publication Data is available.

ISBN 978-0-06-123905-2 (trade bdg.)

Typography by Hilary Zarycky

10 11 12 13 14   LP/RRDB   10 9 8 7 6 5 4 3 2 1

❖

First Edition

for Rosemary Brosnan

CONTENTS

Part Three: *Four Months Later*

"This conflict, which threatens us today, is unlike anything America has ever faced before. It is a Shadow War, against an unseen army. These killers do not attack us openly, dressed in the uniform of an enemy nation. They hide among us, posing as friends, and coworkers, and neighbors—while secretly they plot to destroy us. And so we must be watchful, we must be vigilant, and we must have courage.

"America did not ask for this war. It was forced most cruelly upon us. But of one thing you may be sure: we are going to win it."

—President Root Bainbridge
     State of the Union Message

PART ONE

In the Beginning

Not Normal

UNTIL SHE WAS FIVE, SKY believed her life was perfectly normal.

Her world consisted of her family, their horses, their dog, and sixty acres of beautiful New Mexico ranch land. She knew there was a city, not too far away, called Santa Fe. That meant "Holy Faith" in Spanish. It was where her mother worked. But Sky had never been there. She'd never driven on a highway either, or gone shopping, or eaten in a restaurant. She hadn't been to a movie, or watched television. She didn't have a clue what a computer was. And if you didn't count her baby sister, Mouse, Sky had never even met another child.

Her parents cut her off from the news of the world because the news of the world was so disturbing. There were things you just didn't *tell* a child of two, or three, or four.

So Sky didn't know that her country was at war, or what a terrorist was. To her, 9/11 meant nothing but numbers. And since she'd never heard of the White House, or the president who'd been in it that terrible day, she didn't miss either one of them. She was a little fuzzy on the very notion that human beings could die.

All of that changed one day in late August.

She'd be starting kindergarten soon. Her parents had always known they couldn't protect her forever; she'd hear things from the other kids at school, things that would upset and confuse her. The time had come to tell her.

It was a beautiful afternoon. The family sat out on the *portal*, as they had so many times before. Muddy, their chocolate Lab, dozed in the shade. Ana rocked in the old porch swing while Mouse, cradled against her shoulder, watched the world move back and forth through wide, unfocused baby-eyes. Luke leaned forward, elbows resting on knees, hands clasped, trying to find the words.

The afternoon clouds were starting to build, as they always did that time of year. A cool wind was rising. By the time they had finished their talk, the rain was coming down hard.

That night they held their first blessing.

PART TWO

Seven Years Later

2

Red-Alert Day

Sky slept late that morning. Muddy finally woke her, barking out in the yard. She lay there under the covers for a while, trying to clear her head. She felt sure it was a school day, but the sun was already up.

And then she remembered. Of course. It was a red-alert day.

She sat up in bed, wrapping the quilt around her, and closed her eyes. She took slow, deep breaths and imagined herself standing in a meadow full of flowers—wild purple irises, and yellow snapdragons, and tiny white daisies, and here and there an Indian paintbrush for a welcome splash of red. On all sides the meadow was sheltered by tall ponderosa pines, and beyond them the dark shape of tree-clad mountains. The sky was the deepest, truest blue, and the sun overhead was dazzling. It warmed her face, and her arms, and her chest—all the way down to her innards.

Having captured the vision, Sky began to reflect all that light and warmth back out into the world: loving thoughts, generosity, patience, affection, sympathy, tolerance, humor. Every good thing she could summon from her spirit she offered up as her morning gift.

Then, since it was a red-alert day, she did an extra blessing. Concentrating hard once more, she called the terrorists up in her mind. She always pictured them as young—olive-skinned, teenage boys with curly, dark hair and large, brown eyes. They'd be handsome if they didn't look so angry.

We're not your enemies, she told them. *We can all live together in peace. Please don't take any lives today!* She whispered this over and over again—softly, patiently, like a mantra. When her imaginary terrorists turned to look at her and smiled, she knew her job was done.

"Amen," she whispered, then slipped into her bathrobe, grabbed her clothes from the chair by the bed, and thumped her sister gently on the head as she passed.

"Upsey-doodle," she said, then made a dash to be first in the bathroom.

"Grrrrr!" Mouse called after her.

Sky stepped into the shower and turned on the water.

As she did every morning, she thanked the summer rain and the winter snow that had soaked deep into the ground so it could be pumped out again for their use. And she thanked the wind for powering the water pump, and the sun for providing the energy to heat the water. She remembered to thank her father for putting those solar panels on the roof, and building the passive solar hot-box around the water tank, and doing all that plumbing and tile work on their spiffy new bathroom. She even thanked herself and Mouse for the pretty mosaic—fish, and crabs, and seaweed— they had made out of pebbles on the floor of the shower stall.

Thank you all, even myself, for making this perfect moment possible, this greatest of all human pleasures: the hot shower.

Having finished her final blessing for the morning, and being well aware that she lived in the desert where water was a precious commodity, Sky turned off the faucet, toweled herself dry, and got dressed.

Mouse was waiting outside the bathroom door, wrapped in her quilt and attempting to look fierce. In this she was not successful. That little head, with its halo of messy curls, peeking out from a mass of down comforter—entirely too cute.

"Enjoy," Sky said, grinning.

Muddy, who'd been sleeping contentedly in his usual spot next to the cast-iron stove, hoisted himself up and brought her a pillow from the couch. She thanked him, ruffled his ears, and put the pillow back where it belonged.

Then she went to join her father in the kitchen.

"Hey," she said.

"Hey yourself."

She stood beside him, leaning against the counter, watching bacon sizzle in the pan. That meant there would be corncakes, too, with fried apples on top. The latest version of their special breakfast.

"Daddy," she said dreamily, "remember when we used to have blueberry pancakes and maple syrup?"

"Yes, I do, Sky. I was the one who made them."

"And orange juice?"

"I remember that, too. Also coffee."

All those things were rationed now. Because of the war and the oil shortage.

"Do you miss it? Coffee?"

"I would if I let myself dwell on it."

"I always thought it smelled kind of nasty."

"Really? Well, there you go. Different strokes."

Sky pulled out a kitchen chair and straddled it backward, leaning her crossed arms over the backrest.

"So," she said, trying her best to sound casual, "have you heard anything yet?"

He didn't turn around. "No," he said. "Don't obsess on it, Sky."

"I'm not obsessing. I just asked."

"Aunt Pat will call us if anything happens. And if she

does, I will tell you."

She knew he meant well. He was only trying to protect them. But he went so needlessly over the top, it drove her positively nuts.

"Where's Mom?" she asked after a while. "Is she gone already?" Ana was a nurse; and medical personnel, like all other first responders, had to work on red-alert days.

"It's almost *nine*," he said. "She left two hours ago."

"Oh, shoot!" Sky jumped up from the chair and grabbed her fleece off the peg by the door. She'd completely forgotten about the horses.

"Don't worry," Luke said. "I already fed 'em."

"You did? Sweet Daddy!" She went over and wrapped her arms around him. It felt good, so she stayed there for a while, leaning her head against his back while he went on frying bacon.

"You and Mouse need to do a good cleanup in the barn this morning," he said.

"I know."

"Then we'll shoe the horses in the afternoon."

"Okay."

Mouse shuffled into the kitchen, her curls wet and droopy, her eyes still sleepy.

"Daddy fed the horses for us."

"Oh." Mouse flashed an angelic smile. "Thanks!"

"You're welcome. I explained to Peanut and Blanca that

you were a couple of lazy heads, and they said that was all right as long as it didn't happen too often."

"They're very understanding," Sky said.

"Prince didn't much care. He was just hungry."

"Yeah. Figures."

Luke handed Mouse a bowl of sliced apples. "Spoon that into the skillet and stir it around. Careful, the handle's hot. Don't let the apples burn."

Mouse set the bowl on the counter, dragged the footstool over to the stove, and climbed up. Carefully, she scooped the fruit into the skillet. It sizzled in the bacon grease and gave off wonderful smells.

"Has Aunt Pat called?"

"*No,* Mouse." There was an edge to Luke's voice now. "But she *will* if anything happens. *As you know.*"

"Yeah," Mouse said. "I do. And my friends think it's totally *weird* how we get all our news from—"

"*Fine!*" Luke said. "Let 'em!"

"I wish we had a TV," she muttered, almost to herself.

"You do? Why?"

"'Cause then we'd know if there was an attack or not. We wouldn't need Aunt Pat to call and tell us. Andrea's mom leaves it on all day whenever there's a red alert. They know right away if anything—"

"Great! What a good idea! We wouldn't want Andrea to miss any of that death and destruction. I mean, you can never get enough of that stuff, can you?"

Mouse stared at him, open-mouthed.

"You've seen a big-screen TV, right? Like the one in the library at school?"

She nodded.

"So you know how vivid and lifelike the images are. Is *that* what you want, baby? You want to *watch* people dying? Up close? In *high definition*?"

Mouse made a little growling sound deep in her throat. She threw the spoon into the skillet, jumped off the stool, and ran into the bedroom, tears streaming down her face. Luke turned off the flame under the pan and followed her.

Their voices drifted in from the other room—Mouse sobbing, Luke comforting. Sky waited. After a while they came back to the kitchen. Luke was holding Mouse's hand. They both looked very solemn.

"I'm sorry, Sky. I was way out of line. It's just . . ."

"I know, Dad."

He nodded.

Mouse climbed back onto the stool and started stirring the apples again. Luke reached across and turned the fire back on.

"I'm thinking good thoughts now," Mouse announced, wiping the remnants of tears from her face with the back of her hand.

"Good plan," Luke said.

"I think there *won't* be an attack today. We didn't have one last time. Maybe nothing will happen at all."

Luke stopped what he was doing and went over to Mouse. Laying a hand on each of her shoulders, he leaned down and kissed the top of her head.

"From your lips to God's ears," he said.

When the apples were ready, Luke fired up the iron skillet, melted some butter, and poured in three puddles of batter. He gave the pan a little shake, spreading the liquid out a little more to make the corncakes thinner. They'd never be as fine and delicate as the real pancakes he used to make, with those sweet, gooey berries all bursting inside and the clear amber syrup on top. But they'd still be good.

Sky got three plates out of the cupboard and set them on the counter next to the stove. Then she laid out the forks, and the knives, and the napkins, and filled three tumblers with apple juice.

"Daddy?" she said.

"Yes, pumpkin."

"We *are* kind of weird, you know. The way we do things."

"I guess."

"But I like it."

"Good."

"Most of the time."

3

Professor Frybrain and His Stink-away Juice

SKY DETESTED GERALD.

She'd known him since kindergarten. Back then they'd even played together, at least the first couple of weeks. Sky was a high-energy kid, and he was, too. They'd done a lot of chasing around the playground together.

But after a while he'd started to make her uneasy. Anything he got his hands on—a building block, a carrot stick, a plastic cow—turned magically into a gun; and he would run around pointing it at the other kids, going *"Ptchew-ptchew-ptchew*, you're dead!"

Sky couldn't fathom this, even after her mother had told her what a gun was and explained what *dead* meant. Why would anyone think it was fun to pretend something like that?

Then came that beautiful, crisp November morning

when the famous bridge was destroyed. Sky had been at school at the time; there were no red-alert days back then. The system of safe rooms wasn't in place yet either, so parents were called to take their children home. By the time Ana had arrived, Sky was almost petrified with fear.

They'd talked about it at home for quite a while, and held a really good blessing afterward for the people who'd died. It had helped, but Sky was still feeling anxious.

The next day at school, Gerald had wanted to play terrorist. He'd made a bunch of kindergartners stand on a picnic bench, then proceeded to "blow it up" by making loud explosion noises, and waving his arms in the air, and pushing the kids off the "bridge."

Sky had become hysterical and ran to tell a teacher. Gerald was sent home for the rest of the day. After that she was permanently on his hit list.

He hadn't changed much since then. He was still a bully and a show-off. Teachers still didn't like him. And he still got in trouble all the time. But he was a lot bigger now, and meaner.

Sky had long ago learned that the best thing to do was simply to keep her distance. Mostly that meant avoiding him in the lunchroom and the carpool line. But during class time, when the teachers were in charge, even Gerald had to act like a normal person.

Except, that is, in science.

Mr. Bunsen, you see, believed seventh-grade science should be fun. The more the kids laughed, the better he liked it. Naturally, Gerald and his merry band of misfits, Javier and Travis, were only too happy to oblige.

In Sky's opinion, Mr. Bunsen wasn't nearly as funny as he thought he was. She was hoping that since this was the day following a red alert, he'd turn the humor down a notch—even though there hadn't actually been an attack.

But no. There he was, all smiles, gesturing toward the chalkboard. "Meet Professor Frybrain," he said.

He had drawn a picture of the professor on the board with huge round glasses, enormous clown feet, and hair that stuck out all over his head.

The class giggled.

"The professor has ten students in his class. Yes, Gerald?"

"What does Professor Frybread teach?"

"Fry*brain*, Gerald, not Fry*bread*. And he teaches . . . advanced pineapple slicing."

That got Bunsen another laugh, and he grinned.

"But that's neither here nor there. What we're really interested in today is Professor Frybrain's *problem*. Can anybody guess what it is? No, probably not. Well, it's *body odor*! Not *his*, let me quickly add. No, no—it's his *students* who are stinky. You see, they all ride their bikes to school so as not to use any fossil fuels; and by the time they get to class, they're all sweaty and smelly."

He wrinkled his nose.

"So, what's our poor professor to do?"

Sky heard a plaintive little sigh coming from somewhere to her right and turned to look. It was the new boy, Kareem, the one her mom had told her to be nice to. Actually, what Ana had said (in typical clueless parent mode) was "Make friends with him, Sky."

Ah, yes. Make friends. So easy. Piece of cake.

Hello, Kareem, my name is Sky. I was just thinking, though you're a complete and total stranger, maybe you and I could . . .

She'd given it a try anyway, since he *was* new in town, and it *would* be a nice gesture, and her mother *had* asked her to do it. Unfortunately it had turned out to be just as awkward as she'd expected it to be. The only thing she could think of to say—that her mom knew his dad from the hospital where they both worked—had utterly failed to get things going. Kareem had merely nodded and said, "I know."

End of conversation.

She'd caught herself nodding back at him, nodding and nodding like some demented bobble-head doll. She made herself stop.

"So, anyway," she'd mumbled, "you know, I mean, I just wanted to say hi and all. . . ." It had been so embarrassing. He clearly thought she was an idiot.

But now, in the split second before she turned away, Kareem caught her watching him and flashed a conspiratorial grin. She responded with a subtle eye roll and suppressed a giggle.

Ah. That was better.

Bunsen was still going on about Professor Frybrain, who was now in his laboratory, working and working to solve his problem.

Please, *please* get to the point, Sky thought.

"And then— *eureka!*" the teacher practically shouted. "He invented it! *Stink-away Juice!*"

"Oh, joy," Kareem whispered. Very softly, but Sky knew he meant for her to hear. She responded by crossing her eyes.

Mr. Bunsen drew an outstretched arm on Professor Frybrain—he already had two, this one made three—holding a test tube. He labeled it STINK-AWAY JUICE. Gerald and his pals were snorting, and squealing, and playing drumrolls on their desks.

"The next step, of course, was to *test* his new invention, to make sure it really worked. So he told his class that *all* of them would receive a dose of Stink-away Juice. But . . ."—he lowered his voice to a dramatic whisper—"*only five of them actually did.* The other five got sugar water. Now what would you call the five students who didn't get the real medicine?"

He looked around the room. Rachel's hand was up.

"Somebody besides Rachel this time," Bunsen said. "All right, Travis?"

"Stinky?"

"Well, yes, we could probably call them stinky, but I was looking for something a little more . . . scientific? Somebody? Anybody?"

Sky checked her watch. Fifteen minutes down, thirty more to go.

"Arnold?"

Arnold shrugged.

"Bethany?"

Bethany stared out the window.

"Oh, come *on*, people. Kareem? Any idea what we'd call the group that got the sugar water?"

"The control group," he said quietly.

"Excellent. And the sugar water?"

"A placebo."

"*Thank you*, Kareem. Gerald, what's so funny?"

"Oh, *nothing*," Gerald said, collapsing into a fit of strangled giggles, more of a series of snorts, really, as though Kareem's mere existence—and certainly the fact that he'd actually answered a question—was just so unbelievably hilarious.

Sky recognized the signs. Kareem was Gerald's latest victim.

He was an obvious choice. He was new, and he had a foreign name that Gerald could make fun of. His family had come from the Middle East, so there was the terrorist angle to run with. And best of all, Kareem was smart, and well behaved, and a good student. Gerald had lots of colorful names for kids like that.

"Now Professor Frybrain got out his Smell-o-Meter," Bunsen said. "A wonderful machine, one of his very best inventions—and measured the degree of stinkiness of each student."

Naturally they got a picture of the Smell-o-Meter, too. Bunsen liked to draw. Sky noted that it took up a minute and a half of class time. On the left side of the dial, he wrote FRESH AS A DAISY and on the right, SWEATY SOCKS.

"And guess what he discovered?" Bunsen paused to let the tension build, eyes wide with excitement. Sky wondered if he secretly dreamed of being an actor—or maybe a stand-up comic.

"The ones who'd been given the Stink-away Juice smelled *fresh as a daisy*, while the others smelled like *sweaty socks*. Would you say his invention was a *success*?"

"Yes!" everyone roared.

"I couldn't agree more. A Nobel Prize for Professor Frybrain! Now, moving on, what aspect of his experiment would you say was the *independent variable*?"

Silence reigned in the classroom.

"Come on, guys. Didn't anybody do the reading? Oh, all right, Rachel."

"The *independent* variable is whether the Stink-away Juice was given to the students or not; and the *dependent* variable is the result, which in this case was that the students who got the juice smelled good and the ones who didn't smelled bad."

"Thank you, Rachel. Even more than I asked for. If they let twelve-year-olds teach school, you could take over this class."

"I'm thirteen."

"I stand corrected. Now. Professor Frybrain decided to refine his experiment, giving different amounts . . ."

And so it went. Finally, *finally* the bell rang.

But once that crew got all riled up, it was hard to tamp them back down. Out in the hall, the hilarity continued.

"Yo! Abdool-a-mush," Gerald yelled at Kareem. "Need some Stink-away Juice?"

"Ew, what smells?" Javier made a face.

"*Cut it out*, guys," Sky yelled. "Leave him alone." She was breaking her rule of avoiding Gerald, but she just couldn't stand it anymore.

Gerald stopped in his tracks and stared at her, a smirk growing on his face.

"*Yeah*, hippie-weirdo?"

"*Yeah*, Gerald. Try acting like a person for a change. See how it feels."

"Ooooh, ouch. So is Abdool-a-mush your *boyfriend*? Is *that* it?"

She was about to come back with another smart remark when her eyes suddenly went wide. She'd just been blessed with an inspiration.

"Say, Gerald," she said, "remember that hamster, back in kindergarten?"

"Shut up, Sky!"

"It's a great story. Javier, have you heard about the hamster? You, Travis?"

"I said *shut up!*"

"All right. I will, as you say, *shut up*—*if* you leave Kareem alone. Is it a deal?" She tilted her head and smiled.

"You wouldn't dare," he snapped.

"You sure?"

He gave her a threatening look, then turned and started to leave.

"Okay. Fine with me. Hey, Travis, want to hear—"

"Oh, *all right!*" Gerald snapped. "Deal."

4

The Universe Is One Great Spirit

THE CALL CAME ON FRIDAY night, three days after the red alert.

They had finished dinner, switched off the electricity to save the batteries, and brought out the "endless power" lanterns. They were the windup kind, designed for camping.

The girls were curled up on the couch with a blanket, while Luke sprawled in his big leather chair and Ana sat ready, the book in her lap: *Mrs. Frisby and the Rats of NIMH*. It was reading time.

She was only a few pages into the story when they heard the tones of "*La Paloma*" coming from the kitchen. That was Aunt Pat's ring tone. Luke jumped up to answer the phone.

They waited in stony silence. They could only catch the

occasional word, but there was no doubt it was bad news. You could see it in the way his body slumped, the way he stared at the floor as he listened. Finally he told Pat good-bye, flipped the phone shut, and wordlessly herded them over to the kitchen table. They sat in a circle as they always did, hands clasped.

"There's been another attack," he said. His voice was gentle and soft. "Two, actually. They destroyed some oil refineries and petrochemical plants in Louisiana—"

"What's that?" Mouse asked. "What's a petro—?"

"Petrochemical plant. It's like a factory. It takes crude oil and natural gas and turns them into things we use."

"You said there were two attacks," Sky reminded him. "Did you mean the plants *and* the refineries? Two separate things?"

"No. They also destroyed the pumping system for our Strategic Petroleum Reserve. That's extra oil we have stored underground in case of a national emergency. The oil's still there, but we can't get it out until the system's repaired."

"Oh."

Sky felt strangely unmoved. She knew what had happened was terrible, but somehow she couldn't relate to it. The destruction of a building, or a tunnel, or a mall—that sort of thing she could understand. It had a human element. It was scary. But factories, and pumps, and oil . . .

"What this means," Luke said as though reading her mind, "is that fuel is going to be scarce for a while. Much more so than it is now."

"Was anybody killed?" Sky asked.

"Yes. We don't know how many. They can't get in to search till the fires are under control."

He didn't say anything more after that. He just sat there, a daughter's hand in each of his, gazing meaningfully at Ana across the table. She gazed meaningfully back.

There was more to this story; Sky could tell.

Finally Luke squeezed their hands. That was it, then. He was ready to start the blessing.

"People died tonight," he said. "We take this moment to honor them."

"They were innocent," Ana picked up the chant.

"Some of them had children who will miss them very much." As Mouse said this, she immediately started to cry.

"They had husbands, and wives, and parents."

"Brothers and sisters."

"They were probably really scared."

"We didn't know them, but we mourn them just the same. They walked this earth beside us, and they did some good, and they loved people, and they died too young."

None of them wiped their tears away; no one was embarrassed. This was their gift, their small acknowledgment of lives that had been lived, then lost. It was a sad thing. Tears were appropriate.

They sat quietly for a while, focusing their thoughts on the spirits of the dead, now floating skyward to become one with the stars.

"We send each of you our blessing," Luke said, rising to his feet and leading them out the front door, onto the *portal*. They took their accustomed seats, Mouse and Sky rocking rhythmically in the porch swing.

Ana brought out the blankets; it was already very cold. Then they sat in silence, gazing out at the dazzling light show spread across the sky. So many stars, so many spirits. Millions and millions of lives, begun and ended since the world began.

Sky let her mind travel up to the heavens and imagined each person who had died that night. She blessed every one. *You, and you, and you,* she whispered in her mind. *Good-bye. We will miss you. Be well.*

The blessing lasted about fifteen minutes. Ana always seemed to know when the right amount of time had passed. Then she took up the final farewell.

"The universe is one great spirit," she said. "Every breath you took over the course of your life is with us still. It fills the air we breathe. You have become part of us. You are eternal now."

"Eternal," the girls repeated.

And then, all together: "Good-bye."

They gathered up the blankets and went inside. Ana folded them carefully and put them away in the cupboard. Luke got a small yellow pad out of a kitchen drawer and, leaning against the counter, began to write.

Ana turned to the girls, opening her arms wide. "Come here," she said.

Sky loved it when her mother did this. They snuggled together, the three of them, Ana encircling them in a gentle embrace. Sky could smell her sister's hair. It always made her think of freshly ironed shirts. They swayed slightly.

"That was a good blessing," Ana said.

"I thought so, too," Sky agreed. She'd especially liked the part about the "one great spirit." It had felt very true to her.

"Will you be able to sleep tonight?" Ana asked.

"Yes," Mouse said, her voice muffled by Ana's sweater.

"Yes," Sky agreed.

And it was true. She felt serene and strangely hopeful now. They had blessed the departed, and been blessed in return. And all their spirits were eternal.

With that reassuring thought, she wrapped an arm around her sister's shoulders and the two of them headed for bed.

5

Voices in the Darkness

AT SOME POINT DURING THE night, Sky woke up. She wasn't sure how long she'd been asleep, but she thought she'd heard a noise. Was it the phone? It couldn't be, not this late at night. She must have imagined it. But she definitely heard voices.

She got out of bed, crept barefoot into the hallway, and peeked around the corner. A fire was still going in the stove, but it was the only light in the room. Her parents sat in the near-dark, speaking softly.

"It'll be a lot of work," Ana was saying.

"I know. But I still think we ought to do it."

"The pantry's full to bursting, Luke."

"Yes, but a greenhouse isn't that hard to build, and it'll be good to have fresh vegetables year-round. Plus, we can trade what we don't need for other things: hay and firewood. Meat. Milk."

"Or give it away." Sky could hear the smile in her mother's voice.

"Yes, that, too. A lot of people are going to need . . ."

"I know, honey."

"We have to do our part."

"I agree. Do you think we can get the building materials?"

"I hope so. We'd better be there when the stores open, though."

"What about the girls? Should we leave Mouse here with Sky?"

"I've been thinking about that. It's really tempting. . . ."

"But they're going to find out anyway. And who knows what they'll hear at school. I think maybe it's better if they see it for themselves, while we're there to explain it to them. And if we get there early, and get out before the panic really starts, it might not be that bad."

"I hope you're right."

"Me, too."

"So what can we get, then, of the rationed stuff?"

Ana flipped through the coupons, holding them to the light so she could read. "Rice, sugar, cooking oil, salt—assuming there's any to buy, of course. What's on your list?"

"A lot. All the building materials. Propane. A heater for the greenhouse. Candles. Lightbulbs. Soap. Shampoo. Seeds. Dog food . . ."

Sky shivered and tiptoed back to bed.

6

Goat-Man

WHEN ANA KNOCKED ON THE door to wake them, the stars were still midnight-bright. In the western sky, a fingernail moon hung low over the dark mass of the hills.

Sky turned on the bedside lamp (they were on battery power till the sun came up) and looked at the clock. Four fifteen.

"Dad and I are finished in the bathroom," Ana said. "You need to get in and out, then see to the horses. We're really pressed for time."

"Why are we getting up so *early*?" Mouse whimpered.

"We're going into town, honey. We have some shopping to do."

"The stores won't even be *open* yet."

"Actually, they will," Luke said, peeking in the door. "Albertsons opens at six. So does Home Depot."

"But why do we have to be there when they *open*?"

"Because there are things we need to get, and we're afraid there might be crowds."

"On a *Saturday morning*?"

"Mouse!" Ana snapped. "Enough with the whining. Just get moving."

Sky could feel the urgency in the air. Her parents were anxious; everything was hurried. There was only time for a bare minimum of horse care before they gobbled down a skimpy breakfast, left the dishes in the sink, and headed for town.

It was still dark when they pulled out onto the highway. The sun wouldn't crest the hills for another half hour. Mouse loosened her seat belt and lay down, resting her head in Sky's lap. Soon she was fast asleep.

"Dad?" Sky whispered. "Was there another call last night, after we went to bed? Or did I dream it?"

Luke and Ana exchanged glances.

"Yes," Ana finally said. "Another refinery. In Philadelphia."

"Was it—?"

"Don't dwell on it, Sky. It was pretty much like the others. We'll have another blessing tonight."

"Okay."

Nothing more was said after that, but Sky understood that things were different now. Three attacks in a single night—that had never happened before. The war was . . . she searched her memory for the word she needed. It sounded like *escalator. Escalating*, that was it. The war was escalating.

They turned onto Guadalupe Street, then into the Albertsons parking lot. It was crammed full. Hundreds of people had gotten there ahead of them. They had already parked and were waiting outside the doors for the store to open. On the street side of the lot, near the Wells Fargo drive-in bank, a small crowd had gathered by the ATM machine. There seemed to be some problem. There was lots of pushing and shouting.

"Oh, my sainted grandmother!" Ana said. "Wake up, Mouse. We're here."

Luke found a place to park at the far end of the lot. It couldn't have been farther from the store, but with the flatbed trailer hooked to the back, they'd known they were going to have problems. Luke pulled in and locked the car, and they hurried toward the entrance.

They waited at the edge of the crowd, not wanting to push ahead of the others who had gotten there first. But more shoppers kept arriving, and they soon found themselves engulfed in a tight mass of bodies.

A man could be seen inside, getting ready to unlock the sliding glass doors. Now the pushing intensified. Sky could feel someone's fists digging into her back, urging her forward. But she couldn't move; there was no place to go.

Suddenly Luke grabbed both girls by the arms and pulled them toward him. "We need to get out of here," he said. "Somebody's going to get hurt." They were working their way through the crowd when the doors finally opened and escape became impossible. The bodies moved like a river in flood, rushing fiercely downstream. Luke wrapped his family in a strong embrace and held them firmly. They became a boulder, the four of them, strong against the rapids. The human river flowed around them.

And then it was over. They stood there for a moment, gazing at the spectacle inside: people fighting over shopping carts, grabbing canned goods off the shelves and throwing them into bags.

"I'm afraid to go in there," Ana said.

"I don't think we should." Luke checked his watch.

"Surely they'll calm down now that they've made it inside and are getting what they want. And they'll have to form an orderly line to check out."

"Maybe. But it'll take a long time, and I think the other stuff is more important. I say we skip the groceries for now and go to Home Depot."

"You're right," Ana said. "Home Depot first."

They hurried back to the car and left the Albertsons parking lot, driving south on Guadalupe, past the historic old adobe Santuario with the polychrome Virgin out front, past the Railyard, and the park, and on down the long commercial corridor that led to the big chain stores.

At every filling station they passed, there were lines snaking out onto the street, blocking a whole lane of traffic—except for a few that had signs out front saying CLOSED: NO GAS.

Mouse had her nose pressed to the window. "Wow," she said. "Good thing our cars run on sunshine."

"Yes, honey," Ana said. "But most people still use gas, and things are going to be pretty rough for a while. I wouldn't go around school bragging about our electric cars and our solar panels."

"Why do you always think I'm going to do stupid things? I'm not a baby."

"I'm sorry, Mouse."

"I *don't* brag about our stuff."

"Good."

"But you need to understand . . ." Luke had shifted into his lecture-the-kids voice. Sky recognized it right away. "Lucky as we are, compared to most people, this is going to affect us, too. The long-haul trucks that move goods around the country also run on gas. And—well, with all those refineries shut down . . ."

"*What?*"

"There are going to be things we can't get anymore.

That's why there was such a crowd at the store."

"All those people *knew* this would happen?"

"Yes, Mouse. They figured it out. We did, too. That's why we left so early."

"Oh."

Sky sat numbly in the backseat, listening quietly, turning it all over in her head. The shelves at Albertsons would be empty soon. Then what? Would they just shut the doors, and turn out the lights, and send everybody home? What about the drugstores? What if people got sick and couldn't get medicines? And the clothing stores, too, and the gas stations? With nothing to sell, the shops would all close one by one until Santa Fe became a ghost town. Whatever it was you wanted or needed, you'd better be prepared to grow it yourself, or make it, or buy it locally—because otherwise, you wouldn't be able to get it at all.

"You all right, Sky?"

She must have moaned or something.

"I feel kind of sick."

"Oh, sweetheart," Ana said, "try not to worry too much. We'll manage. We're in good shape, really. It's just going to be a little . . . *different* for a while, that's all."

"I know, Mom, but . . ."

Ana reached across to the backseat and gave Sky's hand a squeeze.

They pulled into the Home Depot parking lot. It was

even bigger than the one at Albertsons, yet every space was taken. There wasn't a crowd at the door, though. The people were already inside, shopping like their lives depended on it.

"Take the girls and go on in. I'll keep circling till I can find a place to park."

"Okay," Ana said.

"I'll get the heavy stuff—the lumber, and the sheet plastic, and the plywood, and the fencing, and the propane. That has to be picked up around back anyway. You get a cart and do the garden center and the rest of the smaller items. If you see something we forgot to put on the list, grab it. We'll meet up at checkout. If I can't find you when I'm done, I'll call you on your cell."

About an hour later, their cart nearly bursting at the rivets, Ana pulled into one of the many long checkout lines. She phoned Luke to tell him where they were. Then there was nothing to do but wait.

Sky watched the people shop and found it disturbing. Everyone was pushing, and grabbing, and arguing. No one was polite. No one smiled. You'd think those were the very last lightbulbs that would ever be sold on the face of the earth.

Who knew? Maybe they were.

A family pulled into the next line over. They were dark-skinned and foreign-looking. The husband wore a beard, and the wife had covered her hair with a lavender head scarf.

They had two children—a cute little girl, younger than Mouse, and a teenage boy. He was taller than his father, his chin already shadowed with a starter beard.

Sky wiggled her fingers at the girl and she lit up, grinned, and scurried to hide behind her mother. Seconds later she was peeking out again. Sky would pretend to lose interest, looking away with her arms folded, then she'd turn suddenly and flash a smile. Each time the girl would let out a squeal and run to hide.

"That's enough, Raya," the woman finally said. "Calm down."

The man at the front of their line finally finished paying, and they all moved forward a few feet. One down, ten more carts, filled to the brim, still ahead of them. Glaciers moved faster than this.

Mouse was draped over the front of the cart, her head resting on a sack of seeds.

"When are we going to *go?*" she whimpered.

"I don't *know,*" Ana said, wrinkling her forehead with feigned confusion. "When *are* we going to go?"

"I don't know," Mouse said. "I asked you first."

"I asked you second."

Sky went back to studying the crowd. She watched in morbid fascination as two people fought over an extension cord. A man pushed past them, moving aggressively through the congested aisle, straight in their direction. He was very large and odd-looking—that was probably why he'd caught her eye. He had a shaved head, and a big gut, and very pale skin. Except for the long, rusty goat's beard that hung from the tip of his chin, he looked like something made entirely of balloons: round, and pink, and shiny.

But clownish though he was, with that bubble face and goaty beard, his expression wasn't funny at all. He looked like—what? Like you'd better get out of his way.

The man finally reached the cross aisle and turned to the left. There was a little blond kid, walking beside her father's cart, holding on with one hand. She was clueless to the fact that she was taking up precious space. The man started nudging her with his cart. She stopped, turned around, and stared at him. The harried father plucked her out of the aisle and dropped her into his cart. Goat-Man moved into the breach.

Then he spotted the foreign family, and something happened to his face.

They're like cartoon eyes, Sky remembered thinking—the ones with concentric circles that radiated outward, going *boing, boing, boing!* And the thought disarmed her so that she was unprepared when the crash came.

7

He's Only a Boy

GLARING ANGRILY AT THE FAMILY, Goat-Man slammed his shopping cart into theirs. The impact was so loud, and so sudden, Sky felt her stomach flip.

The little girl had been mimicking Mouse, hanging on to the front of the cart. The blow sent her flying. She hurt her leg in the fall and began to cry. The mother, shooting a venomous glance at the goat-beard man, hurried to pick her up.

"What's the *matter* with you?" the husband asked. His accent was clipped, precise. "Why did you do that?"

"Because I don't want you people here," Goat-Man said, leaning closer, chin first, squinting with distaste. "Why don't you go back to where you came from? Huh? Blow your *own* people up."

The girl was sobbing, "He pushed me *off*! He pushed me *off*!"

Ana reached out for Sky and Mouse, pulling them to the far side of the cart. Then she leaned down and whispered, "Stay here. I'm going to get help."

"We have done nothing," the father insisted. "We are American citizens. We have every right. So please move your cart and wait in line like everyone else."

"Why don't *you* take *your* blanking cart out of this blanking line before I blanking *knock it over*?"

Even the most harried shoppers stopped to stare.

"No, sir, I will not. We were here first. We're American citizens."

"Yeah, so you said," Goat-Man snarled. "Only, see, I don't really care." He grabbed the kid by the collar of his oversized parka and gave it a yank.

"And here's something else. I not only don't *care* and don't *like* you, I don't *trust* you either. I think maybe this kid is just *dying* to join the martyr's brigade—" He suddenly realized he'd made a joke, so he stopped for a few seconds to snort over it and look around to make sure everybody got it before he went on. "So, 'scuse me, but I want to see what he's got on under that jacket."

"Yeah!" someone shouted from the crowd.

"Leave! Him! Alone!"

It was Mouse, yelling at the top of her voice.

Goat-Man turned and glared at her, his brow furrowed, danger on his face.

"You telling me what to do?"

"Yeah. Leave him alone. You're *mean*!"

Sky grabbed her sister's arm and whispered in her ear, "Shut *up*, Mouse! He could squash you like a bug. Mom's getting help, remember?"

"But he *is*," Mouse said, not yelling anymore but still perfectly audible.

"I said *shut up!*" Sky hissed.

Goat-Man stood for a couple of beats, unsure whether to squash Mouse like a bug or not. The father took advantage of the moment to move his cart out of the line and send his wife and daughter away with it. They were still retreating when Goat-Man returned his attention to the boy. He began tugging at the parka, trying to rip the thing open with his bare hands.

"I'll do it! I'll do it!" the boy said, reaching for the zipper.

"Get your blanking hands away!" Goat-Man snapped.

The father was trying to get to his son, but the line of carts had closed off the space between them. "Please, stop!" he pleaded, trying to squeeze through. "He's only a boy."

A large woman placed herself pointedly in his way, turning her back to him—arms crossed—and refusing to budge. The father tapped her gently on the shoulder, still determined to be polite.

"Please, madam, will you *let me by?*"

Suddenly the woman swung a fleshy arm around and knocked him to the floor. The crowd stepped back and gazed down in wonder. Nobody tried to help him.

Mouse was howling again, and people in the crowd were yelling at her to stop. Sky was frantic. She didn't know what to do. She put her hand over her sister's mouth, but Mouse twisted away.

So there they were—Mouse shrieking and Sky sobbing—when Ana finally appeared, accompanied by a beefy security guard.

"Make way, make way!" he barked, and the crowd parted.

Ana scooped her daughters into a protective hug. "I'm sorry it took so long," she said. "I'm so sorry!"

"But Mommy, Mommy, Mommy!" Mouse kept wailing.

"I know, I know," Ana said. "It's all right now. This man's going to help."

"What's going on here?" the guard demanded of no one in particular—as if it wasn't perfectly clear. The father, his nose bloody, was hauling himself up off the floor. Goat-Man still had the kid by the collar. The boy's jacket was open—the zipper ruined and the lining torn— revealing nothing more threatening than a skinny kid in a T-shirt.

"What's going on here is *this*," Goat-Man said, inflating his chest, trying to look even bigger than he was. "We don't want no blanking Ay-rabs in here. You shouldn't allow it."

The crowd buzzed with assent. They didn't want no blanking Ay-rabs in there either.

"We are legal citizens of this country," the father said. "We have done nothing wrong. I have explained all this."

"Let me see your ID," the guard said. Only he wasn't talking to Goat-Man but to the boy. "You, too," he barked at the father.

The look of surprise on the father's face, and the way he seemed so determined to be civilized and rational in spite of the way he and his family were being treated, caused Sky to belch out another sob.

The father unzipped his jacket and was reaching into one of the pockets when the guard stopped him.

"Put your hands above your head," he barked.

"You asked to see my identification papers."

"What did I just tell you?"

"To put my hands above my head."

"Then do it! Both of you."

And so they stood there like victims of a holdup while the guard, eyes flickering suspiciously back and forth between the terrified boy and the father's jacket pocket, reached in and brought out a wallet, which he dropped disdainfully on the floor, then the small red folder with the gold-embossed eagle on the front. Sky knew what it was, of course. She had one of her own, though she sometimes forgot to carry it. Luke and Ana each had one, as did Mouse and all the people in the store. It was the man's perfectly legal national ID. The guard flipped it open, glanced at it, then slipped it into the breast pocket of his uniform.

"All right, both of you," he said, "let's go."

"But I don't understand. . . ."

The crowd stepped aside to let them through—they even moved their carts out of the way. A few of them clapped and cheered.

"*What?*" Mouse screamed at the guard. "No! Hey, *mister!*"

Ana put her hand over her daughter's mouth, gently but firmly. She was more successful than Sky had been. She was Mom, after all. She also had a bigger hand.

"Sky," Ana said quietly, "I want you to stay here with the cart while I go and find Dad. I'll take Mouse with me."

"No!" Mouse protested, wiggling free, fiercely determined to stand her ground. Ana leaned down and whispered something in her ear.

Eyebrows went up.

Oh!

In a flash Sky understood everything. Ana was not going to look for Luke. She could do that perfectly well from where she was by calling him on his cell phone. They were going to look for the mother and daughter, who were probably cowering in some far corner of the enormous store. When she found them, she'd connect with Luke.

Then—what would they do? Well, most likely Luke would take the family's cart through a different checkout line while Ana and Mouse escorted the mother and daughter safely to their car. Eventually they'd meet up in the parking lot, and Luke would help unload their purchases into their trunk. They'd tell the mother what had happened to her husband and son and offer to help in any way they could.

Sky knew these things without being told. She might not have every single detail right, but she doubted she was off by much. She knew because it was exactly what her parents *would* do. They'd give up an hour of crucial time while things they needed were disappearing forever off shelves all over town. They'd risk the chance of being taken away by the security guard themselves. And they'd do it for a family they didn't even know, because it was the right thing to do.

The crowd was still buzzing over the incident. Goat-Man, having spent his pent-up rage, was holding court, getting compliments and high fives as if he'd just slain

Goliath with his slingshot. Sky turned away. She couldn't bear to look at him.

That was when it hit her—a hard, paralyzing blow. Throughout this entire, ugly episode, she—Sky—had done nothing. *Nothing!* Mouse, all of eight years old, had stood up to Goat-Man. Her parents, right that minute, were helping the terrified wife and daughter.

And Sky? She was minding the cart.

8

Penance

Sky was up on the ladder, a net bag over her shoulder, stripping the last of the fruit from one of their apple trees. These were the hardest to reach, the ones they'd left for the birds.

This was a lot harder than the regular harvest. There was the endless climbing up and down, and scrambling among the branches, and moving the ladder from tree to tree—all for a few measly baskets of fruit. It didn't make sense. Their pantry was *filled* with apples and pears.

But Ana had insisted. Not everybody had an orchard, she'd said. Lots of people would be thrilled to have whatever they didn't need. She'd even told Mouse to cull the windfalls from the ground, looking for any that were only bruised, or only partially rotten. She would cook up the good parts and feed the mash to the horses.

By a little after three, they were finished with the picking, and the project moved indoors. Sky peeled, cored, and sliced the fruit while Mouse did her slow but meticulous best at arranging the slices on dryer trays. Ana presided over the stove, making applesauce and jam.

"Mom?" It was Mouse's worried voice.

"What, sweetie?"

"Will that family be okay?"

"I hope so. Daddy gave the lady his phone number. They can call if they need any more help. I doubt she will, though."

"Why?"

"I don't know. It's just a feeling."

"What about the man and the boy? Will that policeman put them in jail?"

"He wasn't a real policeman, Mouse. Just a security guard. I'm not sure he can even arrest people. Anyway, they didn't do anything wrong. And they had IDs; they're legal citizens."

"He should have arrested the *other* man."

"I know. It was very strange."

There was silence for about a minute while Mouse thought this over. Then she started in with the questions again.

"Maybe we should call *them*."

"We can't, baby. We don't have their number."

Sky picked up the bowl of scraps and carried it out to

the compost bin. When she came back, Mouse was still at it.

"That man was so *mean*, Mom. I never saw anybody be that mean before."

"He was crazy," Ana said.

"But what about the other people? Were *they* crazy? 'Cause they were mean, too. They shouted all this bad stuff."

Ana just nodded.

"Why did they do that?"

"Oh, Mouse, because they were scared, I guess. And worried. And they were looking for someone to blame. It's wrong, it's terrible; but people do weird things when they feel threatened. And once that man started picking on the family, the others just followed along."

"That's stupid!"

"Yes, it is. Very stupid."

"Is it . . . unusual? For people to act like that?"

"I think so."

"Like an asteroid hitting the earth?"

"Not *that* unusual."

"Mom?"

"*What*, Mouse?"

Suddenly Sky burst into tears. Leaning against the cupboard, she slid down and sat on the floor.

Ana turned off the flame under the jam and knelt beside her.

"Oh, sweetheart," she said.

"It was horrible!"

"I know."

"And I didn't do *anything*!"

"Of course not, precious. Nobody said you did."

"No, you don't get it. I didn't do anything to *help*. I just stood there like a stupid lump and watched it all happen. I didn't do *anything* the whole time except try to make Mouse quit yelling."

"Oh, Sky! That man was huge, and he was dangerous. Keeping Mouse quiet was the absolute right thing to do. You were protecting her. And you knew I had gone for help. Seriously—what else were you supposed to do? Come on, be reasonable."

"I don't know. I should've stood up for them like Mouse did."

Ana took her hand and kissed it. "You have a good heart, my dear. You make me proud."

"I should have done something," Sky said.

"I know. We all want to be braver and better than we are. That's how we keep growing."

"You, and Dad, and Mouse—you all tried to help. But not me! Oh no, I was staying out of trouble. I just stood there, watching the cart like a stupid—"

"*All right, then*," Ana said. "What would you like to do?"

"Do?"

"As penance. If you *truly* believe you've done something wrong, and you *won't* listen to me, and you're *determined* to let this eat you up from the inside, then you need to do penance and get rid of the guilt."

"I don't understand."

"Do a kindness for someone. You can't do anything for that family from the store, but there's bound to be someone at school you could help."

"Like with their homework?"

"No. I was thinking of something harder than that. Righting an injustice."

Sky just stared at her, uncomprehending.

"What happened to that family today was wrong. It was an injustice."

"I *know* that."

"But you didn't have the power to stop it. You aren't strong enough to take on a big man like that. You would only have made things worse, and you might have gotten hurt. Mouse might have gotten hurt. But there are plenty of other injustices in the world. Choose one you can manage. Maybe there's someone at your school who gets picked on because he's different. You could stand up for him. That would be a good penance."

"Like, who?"

"Well, how about Kareem?"

"Kareem?"

"Does he get picked on?"

"Yeah. Mostly by Gerald and his friends."

"Do the teachers protect him?"

"Not as much as they should. And mostly Gerald does it when they're not around."

"Well, there you are. Somebody needs to."

"You set me up! You were thinking of Kareem all along. You said '*he*.'"

"True. His father said he was having a rough time. And Monday will be the first day back at school after the attacks. You saw how it was out there today. The kids'll be all stirred up, like the people at the store today. Kareem will need someone to watch his back. Do you think you could handle that?"

"Yes." (Maybe. She hoped so.)

"Stick to him like glue. Make sure he's never alone. Get your friends to include him at lunchtime. Stand by him in the carpool line. And don't be afraid to call a teacher if things get out of hand."

"Won't he think that's kind of weird? I hardly know him."

"Would that be uncomfortable for you?"

"Well, yeah."

"Good." Ana smiled. "It should be. It's penance, after all. Now, do you mind if we get up off the floor?"

9

Saving Kareem

THE LIBRARY AT SCHOOL WAS open and supervised from six in the morning till six at night, to accommodate parents' work schedules and minimize extra driving in an age of gas rationing. Sky liked being one of the "early birds." It gave her time to finish her homework, or use the computer, or just hang out with her friends. It kind of got her geared up for the day.

She dropped her backpack at the usual table, where Stef and Graciela sat. "I'll be back in a minute," she said. "I'm going to go talk to Kareem."

He was an "early bird," too, but he didn't join in with the other kids. He sat alone by the copy machine at the only table in the room with poor light and no view of the mountains.

"*Why?*" Stef asked.

"I'm going to ask if he wants to join our lunch group. Do you mind?"

"I hate to repeat myself, but—*why*?"

"Because people are like sheep."

Sky's friends were used to this kind of thing. As if prearranged, both Stef and Graciela folded their hands and waited patiently for the rest of it.

"See, after the attacks on Friday, everybody's all upset, and scared, and worried."

"Yes?"

"And they're looking for someone to blame. And Kareem, you know—well, his parents came from *over there*. And so he's, like, a natural target."

They nodded. Following her so far.

"Sheep," Graciela reminded her.

"Oh. Well. All it would take is for one person to start something. . . ."

"Like Gerald or Javier."

"Exactly. And the others would just follow along, like sheep, even though they know it's mean and it doesn't make any sense. It could get really bad. I saw something this weekend. This poor family. It was really awful."

"Come on, Sky," Stef said, a little annoyed now. "You can be clear if you try really hard."

Sky sat down and focused. "If we ask him to sit with us, then maybe the sheep will follow *us* instead. And if they don't, and things get hairy, then at least he won't be alone."

"She did it!" Graciela cheered.

"This is serious."

"I know it is. You just make it hard not to laugh sometimes."

"So, is it all right?"

"Of course."

"Good."

Sky took a deep breath, summoned her courage, and went over there. She pulled out the chair directly across from Kareem and sat down.

"Hi," she said.

He looked up from his book. She had hoped for a smile, but she didn't get one.

"What are you reading?"

He showed her the cover. *The Hitchhiker's Guide to the Galaxy.* Some kind of science fiction apparently.

"Is that any good?"

"Yes."

"You know what I really loved? *Anne of Green Gables.*" She paused. When he didn't respond, she rambled on. "Kind of a girl book, though. You might not like it."

Oh, she sounded like such an idiot! But penance was supposed to be painful, wasn't it?

Kareem was gazing down at his hands, folded over the

closed book, one finger holding his place.

"That was terrible about the attacks," she tried.

He looked up, troubled.

"Yeah," he said.

"We went shopping on Saturday. It was really creepy."

"Creepy?"

"Yeah. Like millions of crazy, panicked people buying everything they could get their hands on. We almost got trampled at Albertsons."

"That *does* sound creepy."

"You didn't go out?"

"No."

Now they were back to the silence again. Sky figured she'd better just get to the point. "I was wondering if you'd like to eat with our lunch group. That's why I came over. You know Ben, right? Weren't you lab partners on that sponge thing? And you'll like Stef, she's funny. And Toby's sort of a nerd, but who isn't, right?"

Better to stop there, she decided, though she hadn't even gotten to Gillian or Graciela yet. Why did he make her so nervous?

Kareem, she realized, was smiling.

"Is this about Gerald?"

"What?"

"You saving me from Gerald again?"

"Oh. Well, sort of. I mean . . ."

He waited.

She bit her lip. "We would *very much like you to join us.*"

"Thank you," he said. "I'd be glad to."

"Really?"

"Yeah, really."

"Good."

He thought she was weird. She could tell. She slid down in her chair a little, trying to look like a relaxed person.

They sat there for a while. He wasn't looking down at his book anymore, but he wasn't looking at her either. He was gazing out into space.

"Gerald's a real horse's you-know-what," she said.

"Yes," Kareem agreed, "he is."

"He was like that in kindergarten."

"You've known him for *seven years?*"

"Yup. And what a joy it's been."

"So what was that about the hamster?"

"You heard that? Wow. Well, I wish I could tell you, 'cause it's a really good story. But my lips are sealed unless Gerald, you know, breaks his part of the deal."

"That's very honest of you."

"I'm an honest person."

He just nodded at that and turned away again. Now he was studying the copy machine. She was picking up something odd about him, but she couldn't quite grasp it.

"Are you all right, Kareem?" she finally asked.

When he didn't answer, she decided to wait him out. It took a full two minutes and then some. She timed it by the clock on the back wall.

"No," he said at last.

Her mouth was shaped for words, but nothing came out.

"My cousin was arrested last night," he said.

10

A Really Bad Feeling

IN THE MIDDLE OF THIRD-PERIOD English class, Sky's cell phone began to vibrate. She'd been carrying one since kindergarten, but she'd never gotten a call during school. There were strict rules about that sort of thing. Cell phones were for emergencies only. They were to be kept on vibrate and out of sight at all times.

Must be a wrong number. She held the phone under her desktop and checked.

Nope. The call had come from her mom. And that could only mean something serious: a family crisis or another attack. Ana would never interrupt her at school for anything less.

Sky raised her hand and asked to use the restroom. She could have just told the truth, said she needed to call her mom; but that would have provoked all sorts of questions, and she didn't want to go there, or take the time.

"All right," Mrs. Chavez said in an exasperated tone. "Just don't forget to come back."

Sky tiptoed out of the room. It was a pointless gesture since there was nobody to disturb. The class had already stopped what they were doing to stare at her. By seventh grade you ought to be able to hold it till the bell rang. Or better still, plan ahead.

She hurried down the hall and out the front door. She found a spot on a shady bench and quickly returned the call. It only rang once.

"Sky—oh, thank God!"

A thrill of terror ran through her body. "*What*, Mom?"

"Do you know where Kareem is right now?"

That was unexpected.

"He's in English."

"Oh, honey . . ."

The tone of Ana's voice was alarming. She was clearly on the verge of tears, and she was not a weeper. Something really bad must have happened.

"Something terrible has happened," she said.

"*What*, Mom?" This was freaking Sky out.

"Kareem's father was just arrested."

"His *father*?"

"Yes. Right in the middle of surgery. They wouldn't even wait till we were finished! They sent in a replacement anesthesiologist, said Hanif had to leave right away. Dr. Krohn sent me out there to see what was going on, and there were these two men . . . they had him in *handcuffs.* They just took him away, still in his scrubs. They didn't even let him change—"

"Mom—"

"Honey, please let me—"

"No, Mom—*Mom*! Listen to me! Kareem's cousin was arrested, too!"

"*What?*"

"Last night. In Houston."

"Oh, heaven help us, this is insane. Somebody needs to tell Kareem. Maybe I should call the principal and let her handle it. I'm sorry, Sky; I'm not thinking straight. I shouldn't have dragged you out of—"

"Mom?"

"*What?*"

"The agents?"

"Yes."

"Were they in a silver van? Tinted windows?"

There was a pause on the other end of the line.

"Yes."

"Suits and ties?"

"Sky, *what?*"

"Just tell me. Suits and ties?"

"Yes."

"Because I think that's them coming up the walk right now. Big muscles, not much hair? Real serious looking? One of them has a reddish mustache?"

There was a short pause. "Yes," she finally said.

"What if they're here to arrest Kareem?

"No. Surely not."

"His cousin's a college student. They arrested him."

"Look, I don't know anything about the cousin, but I can't believe they'd arrest a child. They've probably come to tell him about his father. I mean, they'd have to do that—right?"

"I don't know, Mom. I have a really bad feeling about this. And they just walked in the door. There's not a whole lot of time."

There was a pause while Ana thought it over. "You're right," she finally said. "We need to do something. See if you can get him out of class. Tell him to wait behind the Dumpster in the back parking lot. I'll leave right now. I can be there in ten minutes to pick him up. He shouldn't use his phone. It'll be traced."

"Okay," Sky said. She was shaking all over. "I'm hanging up now."

"Go!" her mother said.

Sky snapped the phone shut and hurried back inside. She opened the classroom door and, in a voice as calm as she could manage, said, "Excuse me? Kareem, your mother's here; and she says she's been waiting for twenty minutes, and you're going to be late for your dental appointment."

It wasn't a good story; she was painfully aware of that. Nobody scheduled dentist appointments for the middle of the day. But there hadn't been time to come up with anything better.

Kareem didn't move. He just looked at her with a stricken expression. When the class stopped staring at Sky and turned to stare at Kareem instead, she winked at him, hard. He closed his book, slid it into his backpack, and headed for the door.

"Don't forget to sign out, Kareem," the teacher said. "Sky, you can sit down now."

"Actually, I never made it to the restroom. Sorry!" She winced cutely. "I ran into his mom in the hall. So I came right back."

The teacher gave a loud sigh but waved her away. Sky shut the door and grabbed Kareem's arm, pulling him down the hallway in the direction opposite the main entrance.

"What *is* this?" he asked. "My *mother*?"

"I made that up. I'll explain in a minute, but right now we need to walk as fast as we can without calling attention to ourselves."

They turned the corner, and Sky spotted the band room. It was empty. "In here," she said.

"Okay," Kareem said once they were inside. "*What?*"

"Wait. In the closet first."

She opened the door. It was really more of a storage room, full of instruments and stools and music stands. "Sit back there," she said, pointing to a spot behind a large box. "That's perfect."

"Sky, will you *please* tell me what's going on?"

And so she did.

He sat hunched over, his face in his hands, shaking with quiet sobs.

"We'll do something about this, Kareem. We'll call our congressman, call the newspapers. They can't do this."

"Yes, they can," he said. "They already have. And your parents shouldn't get involved. They might be arrested, too."

Sky wanted to say something, but for just a moment she couldn't come up with the words.

"Go back to class. The longer you're gone, the more suspicious it looks. As soon as the bell rings and everybody's in the hall changing classes, I'll go out the lunchroom door and wait behind the Dumpster."

"Mom said not to use your phone," she said.

"I know. It'll be tapped, and it has a GPS device in it, too. You'd better take it with you. Toss it in a trash can in the hall."

"Okay."

"You might want to wipe it off first."

"Why?"

"Fingerprints."

"Oh, for pete's sake, Kareem!"

"What kind of car does your mom drive?"

"A white Toyota Electra. She'll take you to our house."

"Okay."

"It's way out in the country," she said. "Near Pecos. You'll be safe there, I promise."

She very much hoped that was true.

The Mystery Woman and the Men in Suits

Sky went back to class and tried to act normal. It wasn't easy. "Fight-or-flight" chemicals were coursing through her system, causing her heart to pound and her hands to tremble. Her face was flushed, and she couldn't think straight. So she did what students have always done when they didn't want to be called on: she kept her head down and didn't make eye contact.

Postprandial, Mrs. Chavez wrote on the board. They were studying Greek and Latin roots. "Anybody want to take a guess? Jose?"

"After prandial?" Jose said. "Whatever that is?"

"Right. *Post* is a prefix meaning 'after.' It's attached to a suffix, *prandial*: 'to make a new word.' So what about pre-*prandial*? What would that mean? Stef?"

"*Before* the prandial thing."

Sky looked out the window for at least the fourth time. The silver van was still in the parking lot. Would it be too much to ask for the suit guys to leave before the bell rang? *Pre*-bell?

"That's right, Stef. So, if I tell you that *prandium* is a Latin word for 'midday meal,' can anybody tell me the whole word? What does *postprandial* mean?"

"'After lunch'!" came a chorus of voices.

"Excellent. Now here's another one. Can you tell me the difference between these two prefixes?" On the board she wrote ANTI- and ANTE-.

Hands went up, but not Sky's. She knew the answer. She'd known all the answers. She was an ace at this kind of thing. But she still didn't trust her voice.

"Toby?"

Toby was also an ace; but before he got the chance to prove it, the door opened. Mrs. Chavez slumped with exasperation. And really, who could blame her?

A head peeked in. It was Mrs. Peña, the lady from the front office.

"Sorry," she said, "but Kareem Khalid needs to come to the office, please."

"He's not here. He left for a dental appointment."

"Really? He didn't sign out."

Mrs. Chavez turned her palms heavenward and shrugged.

The door closed, and Toby was called on a second time.

"*Anti* means 'against.' *Ante* means 'before.'"

"Very good. Anybody want to give me some words using either of these prefixes?"

Nobody did. They were too busy listening to the voices out in the hall.

The door opened again. It was still the office lady, but standing behind her was a man dressed in a dark suit. Sky felt another jolt of adrenaline.

"Sorry to keep interrupting, but we need to speak with you in private, please? In the office?"

Mrs. Chavez looked ready to bite Mrs. Peña, but she dutifully put down her marker and headed for the door. "While I'm gone, I want you to write down as many words beginning with *anti-* and *ante-* as you can think of. Okay?"

Notebooks were opened and quiet scribbling filled the room.

Sky wrote mechanically: ANTIFREEZE. ANTIDOTE. ANTI-AIRCRAFT. ANTIBIOTIC. ANTEBELLUM. ANTECEDENT.

What was happening out there, she wondered?

They're asking about the dental appointment, you dummy!

Did Kareem bring a note?

No, Mrs. Chavez would say. His mother came to pick him up.

When did this happen?

About ten minutes ago.

Did his mother come to the classroom?

No, one of the students ran into her in the hall.

Really? Which student?

The door opened, and Mrs. Peña peeked in for the third time.

"Sky Brightman? Can you come to the office, please?"

"I just assumed it was his mother," Sky said. "I mean, she didn't say. It was just some lady. I never met his parents before. Maybe she was his babysitter."

Sky was in the principal's office, the center of much unwanted attention. Mrs. Peña was peering through the almost-closed door. Mrs. Chavez leaned against the wall, hands folded, looking impatient and annoyed. The agents stood watching Sky like a couple of hawks about to swoop down on a bunny. And Ms. Golly, usually so pleasant and cheerful, sat stiffly in her chair, fixing Sky with a look that said she knew a lie when she heard one.

"You were not aware, then, that Kareem doesn't *have* a mother? That she died a long time ago?"

"*No!*" Sky flushed, remembering the look that had crossed Kareem's face when she'd told him his mom was there. Oh, jeez! How to make a bad situation worse! And then, while they were walking down the hall, what was it he'd said? "My *mother?*"

"So, this mystery woman," Ms. Golly said. "What did she say, exactly?"

"Um, 'I'm looking for Kareem Khalid. Do you know where he is?' Something like that. 'He's late for his dental appointment.'"

"Why didn't she come to the office? That's the normal procedure."

Sky shrugged. "I don't know. She just said she needed him to come, so I went back to class and told Kareem she was out there."

"So, where is he *now*, Sky?" This from one of the men in suits, the one with the ginger mustache. He leaned forward as he spoke, resting his big hands on the desk. Sky didn't care for the way he looked at her, or the way he used her name.

"At the dentist's, I guess."

"Did you see them leave together?"

"No. I went to the bathroom. Other direction."

"And then you came right back?"

"Yes."

"Not exactly," Mrs. Chavez said. "I'd say you were gone a good ten minutes. Both times."

Things really got quiet then.

"Ms. Golly," Sky said, her eyebrows knitted in feigned concern, "has Kareem been, like, *kidnapped* or something? I mean, you called in the police and everything?"

She indicated the two men.

This was much, much better, she thought. Definitely more convincing. Plus, she'd managed to change the subject at a very awkward moment.

"No, dear. We don't think he's in any danger. It's just irregular, that's all. Students aren't supposed to leave school without signing out."

The bell rang, marking the end of third period. Kareem would be leaving the band room now, trying to be inconspicuous in the crowd. If the agents would just stay there talking for another five minutes . . .

"All right, Sky," Ms. Golly said. "You can go now. Mrs. Chavez, I apologize for interrupting your class. Gentlemen, I'm afraid I can't give you any more information, and right now I really have to call his—"

"We need to search the school," said the other guy, the one with the shaved head.

Ms. Golly squinted her eyes, catlike. "I'm sorry, I don't understand. *Search the school?*"

"He might be hiding somewhere in the building."

"*Hiding?*"

"Yes."

"And you need to speak to him *why* exactly? Has he committed some kind of—"

"We just want to ask him some questions."

"In regards to what?"

"That's not your concern."

She sat up straighter. "Actually, it is."

"No, ma'am. This is confidential government business."

"Well, you're not doing anything till I phone Dr. Khalid. Mrs. Peña, will you get me that number, please?"

"The father's in custody, ma'am."

"In *custody*? Dr. Khalid?"

"Yes. And, like I said, we need to search the school." He pulled a piece of paper out of his pocket and laid it on her desk. She picked it up and read it.

"It's a warrant, ma'am."

"I can see that." She looked up at him, perplexed. "Let me get this straight. You're here to *arrest a seventh grader*?"

The agent met her gaze.

"We're going to search the school now," he said.

12

Something Weird Going On

THAT NIGHT AFTER DINNER WAS over and the horses had been put to bed, they gathered in the sitting room to talk. A fire was blazing in the stove. Ana handed a lantern to each of the girls, and they got busy winding them up. Then she switched off the electric lights.

"We all settled now?" Luke asked.

Ana nodded. "Mouse, please stop bouncing."

"Sorry."

"All right." Luke took a deep breath. "Well, obviously we have a situation here, and a very serious one. Ana has told me about your father, Kareem, and your cousin, and what happened at school today."

"What?" Mouse asked. "What happened?"

Luke turned to his daughter. "This is a very important, very secret thing, Mouse; and we're trusting you to keep it a secret. Do you think you can do that?"

"Of course."

"Because if you can't, I need you to go to your room so we can talk privately."

"I said *yes*!"

"She's fine, Dad," Sky said. "Really."

"Okay. What happened is this. Some men, agents from Homeland Security we think, went to the hospital where Kareem's father works and took him away. They also arrested Kareem's cousin."

"Like those people at the store?" Mouse's eyes grew wide.

"Yes, exactly like that. They wanted to take Kareem, too, but we didn't let them. Mom brought him here instead. So now he's hiding, and it's our job to keep him safe. That's what we have to discuss now—how exactly we're going to do that."

"Got it." Mouse curled up into a ball, her arms wrapped around her legs, chin resting on her knees.

"All right," Luke said. "Now, we all need to face the fact that what we're doing—hiding a fugitive, basically—is illegal and therefore dangerous. Not just for you, Kareem, but for us as well. I wouldn't mention it except that 'us,' in this case, includes our children; and they will always be my first priority."

Sky winced. Sometimes her father could be so blunt. And

none of this was Kareem's fault.

"It's probably just some stupid mistake. I certainly hope that's the case. Maybe your family has the same last name as someone on the watch list, and Homeland Security is all turbocharged after this last series of attacks. If so, then they'll figure out pretty quickly that they've got the wrong people, and your father and cousin will be released. To be honest, I can't imagine what else it could be. A college student, an anesthesiologist, and a seventh grader—not a very likely set of terror suspects."

"It's not a mistake," Kareem said. "And I don't think it's just about us. There's something weird going on."

"What makes you say that?"

"Well, when my cousin was arrested last night, his roommate followed the van in his car. That's how we found out what happened—Charlie called my uncle and told him. The agents said they were taking Sayed in for questioning, so Charlie just assumed they'd go downtown to the police station. Only they didn't. They got out on the highway and drove all the way to Huntsville—and not to the prison either. They took him to one of those detention centers. You know, where they kept all the illegal aliens during that America for Americans thing?"

"The *deportation* centers?"

"Yeah."

"But that doesn't make any sense, Kareem. Those places

were closed down three or four years ago, when A for A was complete."

"I'm just telling you what Charlie said. There were guards at the entrance. They let the van through, then locked the gate again."

Luke gazed down at his hands, frowning fiercely. In the lamplight he looked almost ghoulish. "It would be a big job to get a place like that up and running again," he said. "They'd have to turn the water and electricity back on, and hire guards, and get a kitchen staff." He paused. "They wouldn't—"

"They wouldn't do that for just one person," Kareem said.

"Oh my God!" Ana's voice came out sort of strangled. "They're rounding up other people. Lots of people. Everybody, you know, from enemy countries."

"No!" Sky almost screamed. "They can't do that!"

"I'm sorry," Luke said, "but they can. They did it before, to the Japanese Americans after the bombing of Pearl Harbor. And it'd be much easier now, with all that information they have in the national ID database. They know where everybody works, where they live, where they go to school, where they shop, who their doctors are. Identifying members of any particular group—it's nothing. A few keystrokes on a computer and they've got a list of names and all the contact information they need. The only hard part would be picking the people up, one by one."

"Luke, stop it! You're scaring the kids. You're scaring me!"

"But he's right," Kareem said. "It's the only explanation."

The room grew very quiet.

Ana finally broke the silence. "Okay. Let's not overreact. I'll keep checking the news sites at work tomorrow. If they really *are* doing something like that, then they can't keep it secret forever."

"Why don't we just go online now and look it up? There might be some mention—"

"We don't have internet here," Luke said. "And we don't have a computer."

Kareem looked stunned. "Why?"

"It's not how we do things."

He glanced quickly around the room.

"We don't have a TV either," Mouse said.

"Then how do you find out . . ."

"Aunt Pat calls and tells us if anything happens."

"Oh."

Ana took a deep breath. "I promise I'll keep checking, Kareem. Meanwhile, we have to think—assuming we're right—just what exactly this means for us."

"It means we're in this for the long haul," Luke said, "and we can't afford to slip up. Mouse, *no telling Andrea and making her swear to keep it a secret.* Okay? 'Cause she won't. Nobody ever does. And *no phone calls*, Kareem especially! Not to your house to see if your dad's been released. Not to your aunt and uncle's to ask about Sayed."

"I don't have a phone. Sky ditched it at school."

"Good. That was smart. The rest of you—no mention of Kareem at all. Not even to Aunt Pat. When you use *any* phone for *any* reason, assume somebody's listening."

"That's totally creepy," Sky said.

"Yes, it is. And that goes for the internet, too. Just because you use a school computer doesn't mean it's safe. Or private. I mean it, kids. Think I'm paranoid if you want to, but . . ."

"We *got* it, Dad!"

"Fine. So let's talk about how this is going to work. I'm afraid we don't have a guest room, Kareem. You'll have to sleep on the couch."

"No problem."

"Aside from that, and sharing a bathroom with four other people, you should be pretty comfortable. You won't have to stay inside all day. We've got sixty acres out here, and the house can't be seen from the road. The property is surrounded by a fence, and the entry gate is locked, so if anyone arrives unexpectedly, we'll have plenty of warning. They'll ring the buzzer, or call my cell phone if it's someone who has the number; and one of us will go down there to let them in. That'll give you time to hide."

"Hide where, Luke?" Ana asked. "If the agents come out

here, they'll do a thorough search."

"Not without a warrant, they won't."

"Oh, honey, they can get those in a heartbeat these days."

He took a deep breath and let it out through soft lips. He sounded like a deflating balloon. "I'll need to build some kind of hidden compartment," he said. "Let me think about it."

"The feed room," Mouse said.

"What, baby?"

"He could hide in the feed room."

Luke considered that for a minute. "Not bad," he said. "The construction's pretty rough in there. I could move a wall out, leave a space behind it. No fancy carpentry needed, not like building a false bookcase or something like that."

"I hate to press you," Ana said, "but is there any way you could do it tonight? We'll all pitch in. The thing is, they might very well show up tomorrow. I don't think Kareem's at the top of their list, but all the same—there are just too many signs that point to us."

She raised one finger. "Hanif and I work together and we're friends. I was very clearly upset about the arrest." Second finger. "Then right after he was taken away, I called Sky—they can get hold of our phone records and it'll show the exact time—then I left the hospital and was gone for over an hour." A third finger. "At the same time, right after our phone call, Sky got Kareem out of class. And the agents know that, because she was called to the principal's office while they were there—"

"*What?*" Luke was horrified. "You're just now telling me this?"

"It doesn't change anything, okay?" They glared at each other for a couple of seconds. "It's just what happened."

"I can't stand this," Kareem said, suddenly getting to his feet. "I really can't. I don't want to get you all in trouble. *Please* just take me home. If they arrest me, fine. At least I'll be with my dad. I really, really don't want to do this."

"Kareem—" Ana's voice took on a soothing tone. "Honey, just before your dad . . . left . . . he saw me standing nearby, and he said—just mouthing the words, of course, so the men wouldn't hear—he said, '*Please*, take care of Kareem!'

"Now think about that for a minute—there he was, at this terrible moment in his life, and his *one* concern was for you and your safety. When I nodded yes, that I'd take care of you, he looked so relieved—like he could handle anything so long as he knew you were safe. Please, honey, stay here for him. It's what he wanted. Do it for your dad."

Kareem sat in stony silence.

After about a minute Luke got up from his chair.

"Sky," he said, "grab a couple of flashlights. Let's go out and look at the feed room."

13

A Hiding Place

BY THE LIGHT OF TWO battery-powered Coleman lanterns, plus the windups from the house, Luke pried the plywood panels off the left side wall of the feed room, exposing the studs and the plywood nailed to the other side, which lined Peanut's stall. Using leftover timber from the greenhouse project and some odd bits of wood from the garage, he built a sloppy but serviceable frame to support a new wall, about eighteen inches in from where the old one had been.

The feed room was ten feet square, two and a half plywood panels per wall. The half panel, attached to the corner stud with self-closing hinges, would serve as the entry door to the hiding place. There would have to be a handle on the inside, for pulling the door open, as well as a bolt for fastening it shut. But Luke couldn't attach them with nails. The panels weren't thick enough; they'd go right through. So he glued one-inch wood blocks to the inner sides of the panels and nailed everything to them. It worked perfectly. And with the molding reattached to the wall and the ceiling—though not actually nailed to the smaller panel—the result was completely convincing. No one would ever believe, walking into that room, that it held a secret compartment.

"I want to try it!" Mouse said when they were finished.

"It's way past your bedtime," Ana said.

Luke flashed a glance at her, then his eyes slid over in Kareem's direction. If Mouse went first, it might take some of the fear out of it. Make it fun. Make it a game.

"Please, please, please!" Mouse begged.

"Oh, all right. But be quick."

Mouse pushed on the edge of the panel with both hands. It swung in only so far before it hit the other side of the wall.

"Hey, *gently*!" Luke said.

But she was already inside, the panel closing after her.

"Where's Mouse?" Sky said. "Omigosh, she's completely disappeared!"

"I'm in here!"

"I can't see her anywhere. She's gone!"

"I'm in *here*!"

"Oh, wow, I was really worried."

"Daddy?"

"What, sweetie."

"It's really dark."

"No kidding. Hold on a minute, Mouse. Listen, everybody; I want you to be very quiet for a minute. Mouse, move around a little. No, not that much. Just like your legs are tired and you're getting restless. Shhhhh."

They all stood in silence, listening to the soft rustle inside the wall.

"Can you hear me?"

"Yes."

"What did it sound like?"

"Like a mouse in the house." Luke pushed the door open. "Okay, come on out. Kareem needs to try it."

"That's all right," he said, taking a step back.

Mouse came scampering out, announcing that it was fun.

"I'm sorry, Kareem," Ana said "I know this is creepy, especially at night; but I think it's better if you experience it now, when you know you're safe and surrounded by friends. If, God forbid, you really do have to hide in there, it shouldn't be for the first time. You'll know what to expect. Okay?"

"All right." His voice was expressionless. He went over to the panel, pushed it open, and stepped in as Mouse had done.

"Wait," Ana said. "Come back out."

He did.

"Go in the other way. You want to be facing the feed room. I doubt there's enough space in there for you to turn around."

"Why does it matter?" Sky asked.

"It'll be easier for him to slide the bolt in. And it's better psychologically. Whoever is searching—you don't want them behind you, you know?"

"It didn't bother *me*!"

"Well, you're extra brave, Mousie."

Kareem turned around and slipped in again.

"Try locking it," Luke said.

They heard a scraping sound.

"Okay. It's locked."

"Now, Kareem," Ana said, "try moving deeper into the space, till you come to a beam. That'll give you something to lean against if you get tired. It's probably not a good idea to lean on the panels."

"Okay," he said again.

"You need to be very still in there. The space isn't all that soundproof, as you just heard. So close your eyes and try to relax. Do you have a mantra?"

"I don't know what that is."

"Meditation?"

Silence.

"Never mind. Just concentrate on something—list the states in alphabetical order, or count backward from a hundred. Try to make the world go away. Take long, slow breaths. When you breathe out, let your body completely relax—"

"I need to get out of here, Mrs. Brightman," he said. "Now, please."

Kareem was very quiet as they walked back to the house.

"You all right, Kareem?" Sky asked. She *did* keep asking him that question, didn't she?

"I guess."

"Was it . . . what was it like in there?"

He turned toward her and stopped walking.

"Dark. Like your sister said."

"Yeah."

"And close. And cold."

"Ah."

"Like a grave."

14

I Saw You Ha Ha

"I HAVE A SPECIAL ASSIGNMENT for you," Mrs. Chavez said. "Any of you ever heard of the Land of Enchantment Essay Contest?"

A few hands went up.

"Well, it's a charming little blast from the past, a New Mexico tradition since the late forties, early fifties. Your *grandmother* may have written one of these things, back when she was in seventh grade. I certainly did. It was called the New Mexico Youth Essay Contest then. They changed it to Land of Enchantment later on."

"What's the prize?" James wanted to know.

"It doesn't matter 'cause you're not going to win. So get that out of your heads right now. This is a *statewide contest*, guys, with thousands and *thousands* of entries. Besides, it's not about winning. Yes, Jason?"

"Then what *is* it about?"

The class giggled.

"It's about learning—about exploring an issue in depth, taking the time to *really* think it through, then exploring it some more by writing about it."

"Can we do multimedia?"

"Yes. You can do anything you want, as long as there's a primary written component."

She picked up a pile of papers from her desk and handed them to the first person in each row.

"These are the guidelines. Please pass them back so everybody has one." She waited till the rustling of paper had died down, then continued. "This is supposed to be fun, okay? And in that spirit, everybody gets an A—as long as you turn something in, of course."

Naturally this got a very warm response—clapping, and cheering, and plenty of smiles.

"See, I think by seventh grade you ought to be mature enough to give something your very best effort—not for a grade but for the simple pleasure of doing it well. Javier, that wasn't meant to be funny."

Sky noticed that Gerald was writing something on a piece of notebook paper. Or maybe he was drawing; she couldn't tell which. He was covering it with his hand. Now and then he'd glance over at her and smirk.

"You have two topics to choose between: 'What I Love

About My Country' and 'What Is the Meaning of Courage?'. They're a bit broad, if you want my opinion, and a
little corny. But that's okay. It'll make it more of a chal-
lenge. Yes, Rachel."

"How long is it supposed to—"

"It's in the guidelines."

Gerald was folding up the paper now, tinier and tinier.
When it was about the size of a spitball, he flicked it at
Sky. It bounced off her desk and landed on the floor.

Mrs. Chavez went to the board. Marker in hand,
she turned to the class. "What would you say good
writing is?"

Jacob raised his hand and said that good writing should
be interesting.

"All right." She wrote it down.

Now that the first olive was out of the jar, more came
tumbling out. Good writing should make sense. It should
have the words spelled correctly and have proper gram-
mar. One by one, Mrs. Chavez wrote all these things on
the board.

"Pick it up," Gerald whispered to Sky.

She ignored him, so he poked Helen, who sat between
them. "Give that to Sky." Helen reached down, got the
wad of paper, and laid it on Sky's desk.

"Anybody else?"

"Um, it shouldn't jump around?"

"That's a good one, Bethany. It should proceed in a logical and orderly fashion."

"Read it!" Gerald hissed.

No, Sky thought. Most definitely not. If she read that thing, whatever it was, she'd regret it to her dying day. "Hamster," she mouthed.

He raised his eyebrows, and grinned, and shook his head. He pointed at the paper again.

"Gerald, do you have something you want to share with the class?"

He looked up at Mrs. Chavez. "No," he said.

Sky moved her hand to casually cover the wad of paper so the teacher wouldn't see. But it wasn't there. To her left, she heard Jose make a little snort. She shifted her eyes in his direction and saw that he was clutching something in his balled-up fist. He was fighting to hold back a grin. Oh, great!

"Thank you," Mrs. Chavez said. "Now, I'd say we have a pretty good list here. I'd like to add my own personal favorite. *Good writing is clear thinking.*"

Jose quietly began unfolding the paper. The only thing worse than reading Gerald's note was having *someone else* read it. With the speed of a pouncing cat, Sky reached over and snatched it out of his hands. In the process, she hit his desk with a thump.

"Sky, what *is* the problem?"

"Jose swiped my paper. I was just getting it back."

Mrs. Chavez looked truly disheartened. "Please," she said. "Can't you just *pretend* you're here to learn?"

Sky nodded and looked down. "I'm really sorry," she said.

Then as the teacher went on about the virtues of clear thinking, Sky slipped Gerald's message onto her lap and, under the cover of the desk, she opened it and read:

Does Sky wear BOYS underwear?

I saw you ha ha

15

Do We Have a Deal?

Sky stopped at her locker to pick up her lunch and put away her sweater. Gerald was waiting there, slouched against the wall, grinning like the python that just swallowed your cat. He was very, very pleased with himself.

"So, Sky. What do you say? Do we have a deal?"

She'd known this was coming since English class.

"I don't know what you thought you saw at Target, but it sure wasn't me in my underwear."

She was playing for time, her mind searching wildly for some way out.

"No. What I saw was you and your mom buying *boys'* underwear. In the *boys'* department. Shirts, and jeans, and other stuff, too. And seeing as how you don't have a brother, I kind of wonder who they're for. Your boyfriend, maybe?"

"I don't have a boyfriend."

"You know, Abdool-a-moosh? Whatzit? He just sort of disappeared, didn't he? I think I know where he went."

"If I were you, I'd seriously keep that hamster in mind." A hollow threat, and she knew it.

"Yeah, well, here's the thing. I'll trade you the hamster for the underwear. Deal?"

"There was hardly anything left in the store." She was desperate now. "We just got whatever they had. Boys' jeans, girls' jeans—what's the difference?"

"Jeans, maybe. Even shirts. But not the underwear. Sorry, Sky. I'm not buying it."

"That was for my dad."

Gerald laughed. "I know you think I'm stupid, but I'm not. Is it a deal or not? 'Cause all I have to do is make a phone call."

She sighed. "Name your terms."

"If you say *one* word about that thing in kindergarten . . ."

"You mean, specifically, the hamster that—"

"*One* word, Sky, and I'll make a call. If I'm wrong, so what? No problem for me. But if I'm right, see, that's a real mess, isn't it? For Abdool-a-moosh. And for you. And your parents."

"All right, Gerald," she said. "Deal."

16

Suspicious Origins or Associations

"THE STORY JUST BROKE THIS afternoon." Ana fished the computer printout from her purse. "I'm sorry, Kareem, but you were right. President Bainbridge signed a National Security Directive—that's basically an executive order—allowing DHS to hold certain people in custody for the duration of the war. Actually, he signed the thing about a month ago, but they've kept it a secret till now. I guess they wanted to get the deportation centers back in operation and start making arrests before word got out."

"What exactly does it say?" Luke asked. "The executive order."

"It authorizes"—she read from the printout—"'the arrest and internment, for as long as is deemed necessary, of any persons of suspicious origin or associations.' It goes on from there, but that's the heart of it."

"Whoa! They could arrest anybody they want with wording like that."

"I know. It's shocking. But the president has the power to do it. And the internment of the Japanese was upheld by the Supreme Court. So . . ."

"It's legal."

"That's what it looks like."

"Well," Luke said, "at least we know the situation now."

"Kareem," Ana said. He was sitting over on the window seat, staring glumly at his fingernails. "I know this is horribly disturbing. But there's every reason to believe your father and your cousin will be all right."

He nodded.

"And frankly, the more people who are arrested, the less likely it is they'll be harmed or mistreated. Your dad's just one name on a big, long list of people who come from the wrong part of the world. Nobody suspects him of anything. Eventually this is going to be over, and he'll be released."

Kareem nodded again, but he still looked down and didn't meet her eyes. The word *eventually* hung in the air.

"That's all we know, I'm afraid. This is a very dark and shameful day in the history of our country." She was winding it up now.

Kareem said nothing. Sky ripped off a loose end of fingernail with her teeth.

"But at least you're safe, Kareem."

Sky nervously chewed at the last few fibers of fingernail that were hanging loose.

"It's what your father wanted."

"Um." Sky finally found her voice. She'd been dreading this moment all afternoon.

Luke turned and stared at her. "Um, what?"

"Um, well, there's this problem. Actually, it's not *really* a problem. It'll be okay, I'm sure of it. Only I thought I ought to mention it. I mean, you need to know and all."

Luke buried his face in his hands. "Please, Sky, just skip the preamble and tell us."

"Well—you remember Gerald?"

17

Moon-Glow

Sky woke to a sound of distress, something between a moan and a scream. It was coming from the living room.

She sat up in bed and blinked. The light of a full moon was blasting in through the windows, almost blindingly bright. Sky had always thought of moonlight—so cool, so pure—as a powerful force for good. Now she turned her face to it, bathing in it, recharging her spiritual batteries.

The cry came again, softer this time.

She got out of bed, put on her robe and slippers, and crept softly out to the living room. She knelt beside the couch where Kareem lay whimpering in his sleep, his legs stirring in rhythmic jerks.

"Kareem?" she whispered, shaking his arm gently. *"Kareem?"*

He flinched, and gasped, and opened his eyes.

"You were having a nightmare," she said.

"Oh." He cleared his throat. "Sorry."

"It sounded really bad."

"It was, kind of. Yeah."

"You want to tell me about it?"

"I'm all right. Go back to bed."

"No, I need to stay here a little longer, make sure you're really awake. If you go to sleep now, the nightmare will come back. You have to stir up your mind a little. I usually go get a drink of water or something."

"Is that a scientifically proven theory?"

"No. But it works for me."

Kareem sat up, wrapping the quilt more tightly around him. Muddy snorted in his sleep.

"Was it about your dad? The dream?"

He didn't answer at first. "In a way," he said after a while. "I think I was trying to find him. I don't really remember exactly."

"It's weird how they disappear like that. Dreams."

"Yeah."

Sky looked over at the window, where a stream of moonlight was shining in, lighting up the tip of Muddy's tail. It practically glowed.

"He's going to be all right, Kareem. I promise."

"How can you possibly promise something like that?"

"Well, it's like Mom said. Someday it's going to be over,

and you'll be together again, and everything will go back to normal."

"When?"

"Well, I don't . . ."

"*Months* from now? *Years?*"

"I don't *know*, Kareem. But the point is, he's going to be *all right*. I mean, he's locked up, and that's awful, but he's not going to be killed or tortured or anything."

"So I should stop worrying about it."

"You could try."

"'Cause my father's just, you know, *locked up*. A temporary inconvenience. A little spot of bother."

"I *said* it was awful."

"You said it was 'awful, *but*' . . . That's like *sort of* awful. *Kind of* unpleasant. Not really all that bad . . ."

"Wow, I'm sorry, Kareem."

"You don't know anything about my father, or what he's been through. . . ."

"Stop it! I didn't mean to upset you. I was trying to make you feel better."

"No, you were trying to make *yourself* feel better. People do that all the time. They tell you everything's going to be all right—only they don't really think it is; they just don't like to talk about the *bad* thing, because it makes them feel uncomfortable. But the bad things still happen, Sky. If you want to help, then tell the truth. Admit it really sucks."

Sky sat nursing her tender feelings for a little while.

"I just want you to be happy," she finally said. "That's all."

"But I *can't* be happy. Don't you get that? I can't *possibly* be happy. My father's in prison; and I can't stop thinking about how scared he is, and how the walls are, like, closing in on him and driving him out of his mind. And I'm stuck out here with a bunch of strangers in some weird, nineteenth-century time warp; and I can't even leave the property, let alone go to school. And I'll be repeating seventh grade when I'm eighteen or something, and I'll never get into college, and I don't have a future. . . ."

He trailed off.

"Go ahead," Sky said, hurt to the core. "Knock yourself out. Don't leave anything out."

"All right," Kareem said. His voice frightened Sky, it sounded so bitter and angry. "My cousin's this sweet little nerdy guy who's never done anything in his life but study, and make good grades, and be respectful to his parents. He's about as big a threat to this country as Mouse is. But they come into his dorm in the middle of the night, and put him in handcuffs, and drag him away. And my aunt and uncle—they practically turned themselves in. Last we heard, they were driving up to that place, that deportation center, to try and get him released. They were going to *talk* to someone there, like they were reasonable people.

And now I'm sure they're locked up, too. And my uncle has a heart condition. . . ."

Sky waited.

Kareem wiped his eyes.

"That sucks!" she said finally. "It sucks big time. It's really, really, really crappy."

Kareem started laughing then, almost hysterically, with tears still running down his cheeks, and strange sobs, and gulps, and moans coming out of him.

Sky reached over and squeezed his hand.

"It's like they were just teleported off to some distant part of the universe, and I don't have *anything* left, nothing at all to remember them by. Not even so much as a blurry old snapshot . . ."

"Do you kids know what time it is?" It was Ana, her small silhouette framed by the doorway.

"Kareem had a nightmare. I was keeping him awake till it went away."

"Well, I bet the coast is clear by now."

"Yeah. Sorry."

"Oh, my," Ana said, going over to the window. "Will you look at that moon?"

Sky got up off the floor and joined her mother there. Ana wrapped an arm around her and pulled her close.

"It's blessing us, Mom," Sky said. "Extra hard, because we really need it now."

"We do, don't we? Come here, Kareem. Grab a little moon-glow to sweeten your dreams."

Sky was sure he would think it was totally stupid, but he climbed off the couch and came over to stand beside them at the window. Ana scooped him up with her other arm. Then they stood there, in the silence of the night, gazing out at the desert all bathed in blue light.

18

Real but Not Real

SKY SLIPPED THE KEY INTO the lock of the *casita*'s electric blue door. Then she turned the knob, set her shoulder to it, and pushed.

"It tends to stick," she said. "The jamb's a little off plumb."

She gave it another good shove, and the door swung suddenly open, sending Sky stumbling into the room. Kareem stepped in behind her.

"Cool, huh? A hundred and fifty years old—or something like that anyway. It's the only building on the property still left from the olden days."

"What was it for? It's so small."

"It was a house. A little house. Probably some ranch hands lived here. It had been turned into a storage room when my grandpa bought this place. Then about ten years ago Daddy fixed it up to use as an art studio. He did all the stucco work and plastering himself, and laid the brick on the floor, and—"

"Your dad's an artist?"

"Yes. He's really good; you'll see."

"I thought he shoed horses for a living."

"He's a farrier, yes. But he's also an artist. Come here. I'll show you."

She led him over to Luke's desk, where a small panel rested on a desktop easel. It was a portrait of a man in work clothes, his face weathered by sun, and wind, and dry desert air. His brown hair was rumpled. His eyes were a strange, pale, washed-out blue that made him look a little demented.

"Your dad painted *this*?"

"Yeah. It's part of his Soul series."

"Is that why the man has a halo? Is he a saint or something?"

"No." Sky giggled. "That's Dermot Brody. He's a pig farmer. But Daddy says we all have a divine spark within us. Actually, I think he just likes to work with gold leaf. Don't tell him I said that."

"I won't."

She pulled another panel out of the vertical storage unit. "This one's Aunt Pat," she said. Aunt Pat had a halo, too.

"Your news source from Albuquerque?"

"Yeah. And this is Ramón. Daddy shoes his horses. And this one—I don't remember her name. She works at the Pecos Market."

Kareem went back to look at the pig farmer.

"It looks real, but not real. You know what I mean?"

"Not exactly."

"Well, he's working from a photograph"—this was obvious because it was taped to the easel, right beside the panel—"but he didn't actually copy it. He used the same pose and all; but the light's completely different, and there aren't as many details."

"Oh. I gotcha. Daddy never copies the light. He makes it up by understanding the form, then figuring out where the highlights and shadows would fall if the light came from a certain angle. Usually the upper left."

Kareem stared at her. "How do you know all that stuff?"

"Daddy told me. We work in here all the time, Mouse and me. He teaches us stuff. He went to art school and everything."

Kareem looked at the picture again. "It's better than the photograph."

"That's because the accidents of light are distracting. He takes all that out and focuses on the figure."

"He taught you that, too."

"Yup."

"He's really good."

"I *told* you."

"It's true; you did. Does he sell his stuff, like in art galleries?"

"He used to. But they're mostly all closed now, since the tourists stopped coming. Gas rationing and all."

"Right."

"So he shoes horses."

Sky crossed the room—it only took a few steps, the *casita* was so small—to a pair of desks that Luke had built, one for Sky and one for Mouse. Between them was a cabinet on wheels, with drawers to hold art supplies.

"So, Kareem," she said.

"What?"

"The painting of Aunt Pat?"

He nodded.

"Daddy did that one from memory. She doesn't get up here from Albuquerque much, so he didn't have a picture to work from. Or not a posed one anyway, the kind he likes to use."

Kareem waited.

"So, I was thinking. Come here a minute. This is what I wanted to show you."

Sky started opening drawers one by one. Brushes, paper, crayons, colored pencils, oil pastels, watercolors.

"We have everything you need. You can work here during the day, while I'm at school."

He squinted his eyes and cocked his head, trying to make sense of this.

"I asked Daddy. He said he'd help. Give you lessons and all, like he does with us."

"I don't have a clue what you're talking about."

Sky crossed the little room again and picked up the picture of Aunt Pat and laid it down on the desk.

"Remember last night when you said you didn't have any pictures of your family?"

"Yes."

"Well, you can *paint* them, like my dad did with Aunt Pat—from memory. Your mom, your dad, your cousin—whoever you want. And then you'll have them to look at, see? So you can remember."

He just stood there for the longest time staring at her, doing something nervous with his hands. Then he turned his face away, his eyes straying up to the *vigas* on the ceiling, then down again to the floor, with its weathered brick set in sand. Finally he took a deep breath and let it out.

"You just never give up, do you?"

19

The Big Finish

MRS. CUNNINGHAM WAS UP AT the whiteboard, demonstrating the mysteries of two-point perspective, when the electricity went off. Power outages weren't uncommon in Santa Fe, though they were usually due to extreme weather: strong winds or heavy snow. You didn't expect them on a bright, clear day like this one, with sunshine streaming in through the windows.

The teacher glanced up at the light fixture, said "Huh," then went on explaining about vanishing points.

About twenty minutes later, while the class was busy making perspective drawings—skyscrapers *with* windows, but not too many because that would take all day—they started hearing voices, and footsteps, and people slamming their lockers shut. "I guess there won't be a bell," Mrs. Cunningham said. "Time to change classes."

It was eerily dark in the hallway. The only daylight came from the open classroom doors, and even that was partially blocked by the students as they passed in and out. There was a lot of squealing and nervous giggles as the kids made their way from one pool of light to the next, bumping into each other, hopelessly feeling around in their lockers for books they couldn't see. It was kind of exciting, and kind of scary, like a fun house on Halloween.

Suddenly Sky felt a hand on her shoulder. She actually went *Eeeek!* "Travis!" she said when she turned around and saw him. "You scared the poo out of me."

"Sorry. I didn't mean to."

"Yeah, right." She scrunched her nose at him—undoubtedly a wasted effort, as dark as it was—and kept walking.

She didn't actively dislike Travis. She just avoided him on principle since he hung around with Gerald.

"Wait," he called, trotting along behind her. She sped up, pretty sure she could shake him. After all, how fast could a guy go in those baggy, gangbanger pants he wore?

Fast enough, it turned out. The trick, apparently, was getting a good grip on the waistband as he ran. "I need to ask you something," he said. "About that hamster thing."

"No way!" Sky said. "Absolutely not."

"Oh, come on!" He was bouncing along beside her, one hand still clutching his pants to keep them from sliding down. "Why not?"

" 'Cause it's none of your business."

"Please?"

"No! Just forget it, Travis! I'm never going to tell you."

"Aww."

"Never-ever-*ever*!"

"Okay, then just tell me this." He dodged in front of her now. "You met Gerald at Alta Vista, right?"

"I met him in kindergarten."

"At Alta Vista."

"Why do you *care* what school it was, Travis? Leave me alone. I'm really, really sorry I ever brought it up."

They had reached the classroom by then. Sky darted past him and slipped into her seat. Travis sat two rows over, on her right, in the "Gerald section." She turned her whole body to the left and sat gazing out the window till everyone had arrived and the class got started. Only then did she swivel around to face the front. She could still see Travis out of the corner of her eye, making funny, pleading faces at her. It was really hard not to laugh.

Mr. Bunsen seemed a little frazzled that day. He'd planned a PowerPoint presentation, but the projector wouldn't work without power. So now he was having to improvise, and it wasn't going well. Not that he was all that funny at the best of times, but at least he usually had something to say.

This raised a mildly interesting question. Did Mr. Bunsen actually *plan* his routines? Practice the story of Professor Frybrain in front of a mirror? Memorize his lines? Do sketches of the Smell-o-Meter at home? She profoundly hoped not. It would just be too sad.

He was standing up front, giving a disjointed description of the diagrams they *would* have seen if the PowerPoint had been working, when Ms. Golly opened the door and put him out of his misery.

She looked a little frazzled, too.

"Everybody needs to go down to the safe room," she said. "But *relax*—we're in absolutely *no danger.* We're only going down there because it's school district policy."

Samantha raised her hand but didn't wait to be called on. "Has there been another attack, Ms. Golly?"

"Yes," she said. "I'll give you the details downstairs. I have to notify all the classes in person, with the PA system down. But *everything's fine*; just head on down there, and I'll see you in a little bit."

They all grabbed their cell phones but left their backpacks behind, as they'd been instructed during practice drills. Then they formed an orderly line and proceeded along the hallway, and down the stairs, to the safe room.

In its previous incarnation, this had been a basement storage area. Now it was fully equipped, according to district code, with everything the students might possibly need to be safe and comfortable during a national emergency. The walls were reinforced, the door was blast-proof, and the temperature-controlled circulating air was filtered. There was plush carpeting for the kids to sit on, plus blankets, food, and water in case they had to be there for a while. A generator kept the lights running and powered the TV. Over in the corner was a communication hub with a landline phone and a fancy ham radio.

Despite the bright lights and the cheerful colors of the carpeting and walls, Sky found the room unnerving. It had a stark, empty feel about it. And there was no forgetting the reason they were there: to be safe. Because maybe, just maybe, the bottom was about to fall out of the world.

Sky found her assigned place, sat cross-legged on the floor, and pulled out her phone. More than anything in the world she wanted to hear her mother's voice.

"I'm not getting a connection," Graciela said. She leaned over and peered at the screen on Sky's phone. "Crap. You don't have any bars either," she said.

"Don't cell phone towers have battery backup?" This from Toby, who was sitting behind them.

"I have no idea," Sky said, slipping the phone into her pocket and staring sullenly at the wall. She knew the principal had said they were safe, but not being able to make a call—somehow that was more than she could bear. She had to work hard just to hold back the tears.

Ms. Golly came in with the last group. She shut the door behind her with a heavy, metallic *thump*.

"Finish your calls, everybody," she said. "Quick-fast. I need your attention."

"The phones aren't working, Ms. Golly."

"Then you might as well put them away. We'll use the landline in a little bit to try and get through to your parents."

She waited as phones were flipped shut and the hubbub died down.

"First, I want to say this *one more time*: the attacks were *not* local. We're in absolutely *no* danger. We could just as easily—and a lot more comfortably—have held this meeting in the gym. But we have to follow district protocol, so here we are."

They understood.

"It took me a while to find out what's going on, but here's the story, so far as I know it. The terrorists took out some critical high-voltage electrical-transmission towers. So the power grid is down over most of the country right now. They say it's going to take a while to get things up and running again—weeks, maybe months."

There was a lot of murmuring. Hands went up.

"Hold on a minute. Let me finish. There's more, I'm afraid. They also destroyed some natural gas pipelines. Again, the big, important ones."

"With bombs?"

"Yes, they blew them up. So the bottom line is, natural gas will be very scarce for a while; and that's on top of the oil shortage."

The anxiety level was rising dramatically in the room. Everybody started shouting questions now.

Ms. Golly held up her hands until the kids quieted down.

"Look, I have to be honest with you. This is a big deal. It's going to change our everyday lives. If natural gas isn't available, and the power stays off, we won't be able to heat our homes—or the school, for that matter."

"What about hot water?"

She shook her head. "Sorry," she said. "Same thing. I'm afraid there are a lot of conveniences we'll all have to learn to live without. But—"

"How are we going to cook our food?"

"I don't know. Over a grill in the backyard. Listen, do you want to hear the rest of this or not?"

She waited until the talking stopped.

"Okay. Now here's the other thing about natural gas. We use it to run many of our power plants, which brings us back to electricity again. They've hit us with a triple whammy here—with oil and gas in short supply, and the transmission lines down. It'll take a lot to get up from a blow like that. I'm told that even when the towers are repaired, the electricity won't stay on all the time. It's called rolling blackouts: periods when the power is off, and periods when it's on."

"For how long?" someone shouted.

"I don't know. For quite a while, I'd imagine."

Over in the far corner, near the door, a girl started sobbing. It was sudden and uncontrollable, and within seconds hysteria began to spread through the room.

"Boys and girls!" Ms. Golly shouted. "Calm down. It's not that bad! I don't like this any more than you do, but people have done without electricity for thousands and thousands of years. Socrates did it, and Galileo, and Shakespeare, and George Washington—they all managed just fine. *You* can, too."

"No! That's not *it*!" the girl wailed. "It's all these attacks. . . . Why are there *so many*? They just keep coming. . . ."

"I know, I know. It's scary."

Heads nodded all around the room.

"But you need to keep telling yourself, *this is temporary*. And I don't just mean the power outage—I mean the war itself. Wars don't last forever, and this one's been going on for a long time. Eventually it has to end. And . . . well, this is just my own personal theory, but I'm going to share it with you anyway.

"You've all watched fireworks on the Fourth of July, so

you know how it goes. You're sitting there on your lawn chair, or lying on a blanket, and the fireworks start. The rockets go shooting up into the sky one or two at a time and go *boom*, and then a few seconds later here comes another one. It goes on like that for about half an hour. Then suddenly they start coming thick and fast, *booom, boom, ba-boom-boom-boom-boom, boom-boom!* Right?"

There were a few giggles. The *boom, boom, ba-boom* part was kind of funny.

"And *that's* when you know that the fireworks are almost over. It's the big finish."

Now there was absolute dead silence in the room.

"As I said, this is just a theory, but it makes a lot of sense. The terrorists *have* to be running out of people who are willing to give their lives to do such horrible things. Frankly, I think it's amazing that they've kept it up this long. So I think what we're seeing now—all these attacks, one after another, so close together—I think this is *their* big finish."

Ms. Golly paused for a moment.

"I think it's almost over, guys," she said.

20

A Perfect Day

"Kareem," Sky whispered. "Wake up."

"What time is it?"

"I don't know. I was so excited I forgot to look."

He turned to face the back of the couch and put the pillow over his head.

"Come on, Kareem. There's something I need to show you."

"It's the middle of the night, Sky. Why aren't you asleep like everybody else?"

"It was too quiet. It woke me up."

He removed the pillow and sat up.

"The *quiet* woke you up?"

"Yeah. Listen."

They did.

"Okay, so it's quiet. But it *woke you up*?"

"What can I say? It did."

"Sometimes you can be really strange, you know?"

"Yeah. People tell me that all the time."

Muddy awoke from whatever luscious dog-dream he'd been enjoying. He looked around, a little confused by the lateness of the hour and the undeniable fact that people were in the room, awake and talking. Time to go to work, then, never mind how dark it was. He hoisted his arthritic frame from his sleeping spot and began his search for a likely object. At the foot of the couch he found a shoe and trotted over to offer it to Sky.

"That's a good boy," she crooned, then handed the shoe to Kareem. "I believe this is yours."

"Why does he keep *doing* that?"

"He's a retriever. It's in his blood. He can't help himself."

Kareem groaned. "I live with crazy people who have crazy dogs."

"Just one dog. You awake now?"

"What do you think?"

"Good. Then you have to come see."

She offered him her hand and he took it. Then she led him over to the window, where they stood side by side, gazing out.

"Now, isn't that something?" she said.

The snow had been falling for hours already—fat, heavy

flakes, coming straight down, with no wind at all. It had transformed the familiar landscape into a vision of white perfection, the edges smoothed out, the shapes simplified, and everything glowing in the light of the moon shining dimly through a veil of clouds and snow.

It was like the world had just that minute been created, and no one had touched it yet.

"That's the best thing I ever saw," Kareem said.

"I know. Isn't it amazing? And guess what else."

"What?"

"Do you know what day this is?"

"Sunday?"

"It's the eve of the winter solstice, Kareem. A very special day. The *exact* moment when the earth begins to shift from darkness to light. And after all these months without any snow—and here it is December, and we usually get our first winter storm in October—then here comes this huge, gorgeous, perfect snowfall. And it arrives on *this particular day*. It *has* to mean something, don't you think?"

"*Mean* something?"

"Yeah. Maybe it's like Ms. Golly said—about the war and everything coming to an end. Remember, I told you? About the fireworks and all?"

He nodded.

"Well, what if the season for killing and hating is over? And the world is moving on to something new, moving toward the light. And the snow—it's a promise. A blessing."

"I don't understand the logic of that, but it's a really nice thought. I hope you're right."

"I think I am. And you know what else?"

"I never do, Sky. Just tell me."

"This is going to be a perfect day."

21

The Sled

AND IT WAS.

By early afternoon the clouds had vanished and the sky had turned a deep, winter blue. The sun, so intensely bright in the thin mountain air, made twenty degrees feel warm. And all around them in that dazzling light, the crystalline snow sparkled like glitter.

They had finished all their chores by then. Luke had twice gone up on the roof to sweep the solar panels clean, while the kids shoveled the walkway. The horses' drinking trough was clear of ice, and the roofs of the greenhouse and the chicken coop had been knocked free of snow. Now it was time to play.

While Sky was out in the barn saddling Blanca, Luke went to the toolshed for the blue plastic sled and a length of nylon rope. He fed the line through the pull-rope in the front, making sure both sides were of equal length. Then he set it in place with a knot. When Sky brought out the horse, Luke began attaching the loose ends of the rope to the saddle, one on each side.

"Ever ridden on a sled before?" he asked Kareem. He was tugging hard, making sure his knots were secure.

"He's never even seen snow before!" Mouse said.

"Ah. Well, now's his chance."

Kareem made an inscrutable sound—sort of *I'm not sure* mixed with *I don't think so.*

Luke responded with a quizzical lift of the eyebrows.

"I'll watch," Kareem finally said.

"That's fine. But there's nothing to it. All you have to do is hold on."

"I know."

"It's easy," Mouse said.

"I know."

"And really, really fun!"

"He *knows!*" Sky said. "Shut up, Mouse, and let him be."

She shrugged. "Fine. Then I get first dibs."

"Okay," Sky agreed, "but I want to drive. Can I, Daddy? Please?"

Luke didn't answer. He just looked at her, thoughtfully.

"I know how."

"I'm well aware of that."

"So?"

"No funny stuff?"

"Absolutely."

"Positively?"

"It's a promise."

"All right."

Sky climbed up into the saddle, while Mouse settled herself on the sled and grabbed the handles good and tight.

"Are you ready," she asked.

Ana came out of the house just then and stood on the *portal,* watching. "You girls be careful now!" she called.

"We will!"

And off they went, down the snow-covered drive, rapidly picking up speed. When they reached the front gate, Sky turned off to the right and up a shallow slope, then made a wide loop around a clump of trees, wound through the orchard, and headed back up the driveway again, moving at a good clip now.

"Rock and roll!" Mouse shouted.

"No."

"Please!"

"No!"

"Please!"

"Daddy'll kill me."

"Come on, Sky. *Please!*"

"Oh, all right."

Sky turned to the left, then to the right, then to the left again. Mouse went sliding all over the place, narrowly missing a tree, some brush, the dog. She squealed and shrieked with joy.

Sky turned and looked back at her sister. "Dump and thump?"

"Yes!" came the answer.

Just short of the house, Sky made a sharp turn. The sled tipped over, and Mouse went rolling off, laughing hysterically.

It was a huge mistake, of course. Sky had known this even while she was doing it—only she'd been swept up in the moment, and Mouse was having such a good time.

"Get down!" Luke roared.

"It's okay, Daddy," Mouse said, brushing herself off. "It was my idea. I *asked* her to."

"She *begged* me to."

"It's fun!"

"It's *dangerous*," Ana snapped.

"I won't do it again. I promise."

"That's true," Luke said. "You won't. Hop on down, now."

"Daddy, *please?*"

He gave her the famous *look*, and Sky dismounted.

"*See*," she hissed at Mouse. "What'd I tell you?"

"You said he'd kill you." She shrugged.

"I didn't mean *literally*, you dope!"

"That's enough," Luke said. "Kareem? Want to try it? A better driver this time?"

He shook his head. "I'll go next."

"Can't say I blame you, after that. Sky?"

"Okay," she said, a little sullenly, and took her sister's place on the sled. Luke waited while she arranged herself, feet braced, hands gripping tightly.

"You all set?" Luke asked.

She nodded.

"You sure?"

"Yes!" she crowed. "Let's *move* this thing!"

"All right, then. Watch, my children, and ye shall learn. *This* is how it's done."

He urged the horse forward till the sled was directly behind him and both ends of the rope were pulled taut. He gave Blanca a nudge and they moved slowly down the drive, advancing to a fast walk, then a trot. Luke looked over his shoulder at Sky.

"Ready?"

She nodded.

"All righty, then!"

Blanca took off, nostrils flaring, hooves pounding. Snow flew into Sky's face; the wind blew it away. Muddy loped along beside them, barking joyfully. And Sky could feel the ground beneath the sled, and the thrill of going fast and of not being quite in control—and she felt a wild rush of perfect happiness.

"Turning now," Luke called; and she leaned into it, feeling the sled rise up as it left the drive, out among the trees, toward the barn, around it. They circled the *casita* and the big clump of junipers—heading straight for a small mound covered with snow.

"Daddy, *no!*" she screamed. "The manure pile!"

Luke laughed, skirting the mound gracefully, then headed back down the driveway again.

"Want to go faster?"

"Yes!"

He gave Blanca a good kick, and she broke into an easy canter. They were racing along, Sky almost blinded by the flying snow, when Luke reined in the horse and slowed her to a trot. Muddy dashed between the horse and the sled—a narrow, terrifying miss—and ran, barking wildly, toward the gate.

"Be right back," Luke yelled, and waved his arm. Then he made an abrupt turn around a copse of piñons and cantered back up to the house.

Sky had been looking straight ahead. It helped her maintain her balance and gave her warning of what was coming next. But when the dog ran off, and Luke shouted, she'd glanced over at the gate.

It was only a flash, but she was sure of what she'd seen. A silver van, parked at the entrance. And a man in a dark coat, with a shaved head, his hand on the buzzer.

22

A Few More Questions

"THEY'RE AT THE GATE."

Luke dismounted quickly and handed the reins to Mouse.

"The agents?" Ana unconsciously put her hand to her heart.

"Yes. Get Kareem into the hiding place, fast. Girls, unhitch Blanca and put her away. I'm going back down there to let them in."

With nervous hands, Sky began untying the rope on one side of the saddle while Mouse worked on the other. The knot was tight, and Sky was trembling; she couldn't seem to control her fingers. She made a growling sound of frustration.

"What's the matter?"

"Shut up, Mouse."

Finally the knots were undone. While Mouse went off to put away the sled, Sky led Blanca back to the barn.

Kareem was already in his hiding place. The panel was closed, and Ana had shoved the blanket box up against it. Now she was wiping out the drag marks with her feet.

"You missed a spot," Sky said, pointing.

"Thanks." Ana made another pass.

"Mom?"

"What, honey?"

"You won't forget our story."

"No."

"'Cause they might split us up, you know. Question us separately. And if you say one thing and I say something different—"

"I *remember*, honey. We've been over this already."

"Okay."

From inside the wall, Kareem coughed.

"Shoot!" Ana said. "It's the dust. Sky, get those cough drops out of the tack room. Quick as you can! They're coming."

By the time she was back, Ana had pulled the chest out from the wall and the panel was open a crack. She could see Kareem's face in the shadows. Sky handed the box to her mom, who shook five or six jewel-like hard candies onto her palm.

"Here," she said, giving them to Kareem. "Put these in

your pocket. Keep sucking on them if you need to."

He nodded and pushed the panel shut. Sky heard the bolt slip home.

"Give me one, too," she said.

Ana looked surprised, but she fished one out and handed it over.

"They smell, Mom. Like cherries. If the agents smell it on me, then they won't be curious about it. We'll leave the box on the shelf, in plain sight, and I'll cough a lot."

"Smart girl," Ana said. "Now give me a hand."

They slid the blanket chest back into place and skated around the room, scuffing the floor, erasing footprints and drag marks again.

A car door slammed outside, then a second and third one followed: two agents plus Luke, who had ridden back to the house in the van. Mother and daughter exchanged a look of sudden panic. They scanned the room for anything that might be amiss. But there was nothing.

"All right," Ana said. "Go get Blanca unsaddled. I'm heading back to the house to work on dinner. We'll just try to act normal."

"Okay."

Sky removed Blanca's bridle and replaced it with a halter. By the time Luke came into the barn, accompanied by one of the agents, she had the horse tied up in the breezeway and had put the bridle away.

"Sky," Luke said, "this man wants to speak with you. He's an agent with Homeland Security."

It was the one with the mustache and the meaty hands.

"I met you before."

"Yes," he said. "Last month, at your school. I have a few more questions to ask you."

"Okay." She continued unbuckling the girth on Blanca's saddle. She really didn't want to stand there looking the man in the eye.

"We're fine here, Mr. Brightman. Thanks."

"Pardon?"

"You can go on inside."

"Sorry, but if you're going to question my daughter, I insist on being present."

"Hold on just a minute," Sky said. She carried the saddle into the tack room and set it on the saddle stand. Then she came back for the blanket.

"Sorry," she said, disappearing into the tack room again, returning this time with a towel and the grooming bucket.

"Are you finished?" the agent asked.

"Yeah," she said. "For the moment. Go ahead, ask."

She set to wiping Blanca down, moving around the horse so she'd be out of view as much as possible.

"All right," he said. "When we spoke to you before, you said you left class to go use the restroom. Then you came back and said Kareem's mother had arrived to take him to the dentist. You were gone for ten minutes according to your teacher—yet you still hadn't made it to the restroom. See, I'm wondering about that. Seems like kind of a long time for what had to be a short conversation. What else were you doing?"

"I was talking to my mom on the phone."

The agent looked startled, as well he might. This was a totally different story from the one she'd told at school. But Sky knew what she was doing. She was spinning her new time line, the one she'd spent hours working out that night after the family meeting. It explained everything— the phone calls, Ana's absence from the hospital, even the reason why she'd lied.

"*Really?*" the man said. "That's not what you—"

"She called to say I'd left my arts paper in the car. I gave it to my sister to read, and then when we got to school, I forgot to ask for it back. Mom noticed it when she got to the hospital and was getting her coat out of the backseat. And it's a lucky thing, too, because the paper counts for a third of our grade, and Mrs. Cunningham *hates* excuses. It was really good, too. I got an A on it."

"That's not what you told your teacher, Sky. You said you were going to the bathroom. You said the same thing in the principal's office, too. Want to explain that?"

"Isn't it obvious?" She hung the wet towel on a hook

and got a brush out of the grooming bucket.

"No."

"We aren't allowed to use our phones in school. They're for emergencies only. And my mom knows that perfectly well, so when I saw that she'd called, I figured it had to be something, you know, really serious. Maybe another terrorist strike, or an accident, or a heart attack, or—"

"You couldn't just tell the teacher that?"

"Yeah, and then whatever my mom was calling about, I'd have to stand there in front of the whole class and take the call. You don't have kids, do you?"

"My personal life is—"

"That's what I thought."

"Sky!" A warning from Luke.

"Sorry." She moved over to Blanca's other side, brushing away. The agent followed, keeping her in sight.

"How did your mother sound when she called?"

"I don't know what you mean."

"Was she calm? Agitated? Upset?"

"Irritated, I guess."

"Irritated?"

"I'm supposed to be responsible for my own stuff. She was annoyed."

"And she didn't mention anything that had happened at the hospital?"

"Like what?"

"Like Kareem's father being taken into custody."

"No! Our parents *never* tell us bad stuff like that. They're trying to protect us." She grinned at Luke, but he just stood there stone-faced.

The agent cleared his throat. "All right," he said, "let's move on. So you went out to take the call, heard about this paper you'd left in the car, then ran into the woman on the way back."

"Right."

"Did she say she was Kareem's mother?"

"No. I assumed that's who she was. Didn't I tell you this at school?"

"Just answer the question."

"I already did."

"Can we wrap this up soon?" Luke said.

"We'll finish when we're finished, Mr. Brightman." The agent shot Luke a hostile look.

"So after you called Kareem out of class, you saw him leave with the woman?"

"No. She said she'd wait for him out front. I was going in the other direction."

"All right. So then you went for your unusually long visit to the bathroom, after which you returned to class."

"No."

"*No?*" He was clearly exasperated now.

"I went for my extremely *short* visit to the bathroom,

then I went outside to wait for my mom."

"To wait for your mom."

"She was bringing my *arts paper* over. The one that counted for a third of my grade and was very, very good. Remember?"

"So that's it? The whole story?"

"Unless you want to know what I had for lunch."

He looked at her with ice in his eyes. Sky turned away.

"That's all for now," he said. "But we'll need to search the property."

"You have a warrant?"

"I do." The agent handed it to Luke. "You know, we're not the enemy, Mr. Brightman. *They're* the ones who go around blowing things up."

Luke didn't respond to that, just studied the warrant quietly for a minute. "Can you tell me exactly what we're suspected of?"

"Hiding a fugitive," the agent said. "Which is a criminal offense, in case you weren't aware of that."

"I see. And the fugitive you're referring to—that would be the child who is missing from my daughter's school?"

"You know who we're looking for, Mr. Brightman." He stared down at his feet then, just for a second. Was he maybe a little *embarrassed*?

Luke handed the warrant back to the agent. "Have at it," he said.

"Any of those outbuildings locked?"

"The *casita*."

"The key, please?"

Luke reluctantly took a ring of keys out of his pocket, and removed one, and handed it to the agent.

"Please don't handle any of the paintings. Or the art materials."

"We'll be careful. Now, why don't you both just go on inside and wait? We'll let you know as soon as we're done."

"I'm not finished yet," Sky said.

The agent sighed. "Fine. Just keep out of my way."

"I will. You can go inside, Daddy. I'm okay. Really."

Luke was about to say something when Blanca, bless her heart, lifted her tail. *Plop, plop*, she did what horses do, barely missing the agent's shoes.

For a moment he just stood there, staring in disgust.

"Oops," Sky said.

23

Hunted

Sky was determined to stay in the feed room with Kareem as long as the agent was there. The horses needed to be fed, but that wouldn't take very long. She'd just have to invent some other chores. The agent would never know the difference.

He had started his search in the tack room. Sky joined him there briefly, throwing the towel into the laundry basket and putting away the grooming bucket. She watched for a few seconds as he nosed around—opening cupboards, looking under the saddle stands—then left and went to the feed room.

She coughed theatrically a couple of times, popped another cough drop into her mouth, and got busy preparing dinner for the horses.

She set three plastic buckets on the counter and filled

each one with alfalfa pellets, adding a splash of oats. Then she measured out the salt and trace minerals and added them to the mix. The whole time, she pointedly made a lot of noise—opening and closing bins (*thump!*), unscrewing lids (*cherk-cherk-cherk*), setting jars back on the shelves (*clump*). That way, she figured, if Kareem sneezed, or rustled, or breathed too heavily, the agent wouldn't hear.

She grabbed the red pail and carried it off to Blanca's stall. Normally she would have taken Prince's bucket at the same time. Saved herself a trip. But efficiency wasn't her goal just then. She was running out the clock.

When she came back to the feed room for the last bucket, the agent was in there, searching. Sky sniffed, and coughed, and sucked loudly on her cherry drop; but he ignored her. He was too busy peering into feed bins, running his hands through the alfalfa pellets, feeling around in the oats. Could he possibly imagine that someone would hide in *there*?

Sky grabbed the green bucket, took it to Peanut, and was back in less than a minute. The agent had finished with the bins by then. He was squatting down now, the chest open, pulling out blankets and setting them on the floor.

Her heart began to race. In order to open the lid all the way, he'd pulled the chest away from the wall. And they'd moved it in there for a reason—they wanted to cover that particular section of the molding that ran along the bottom of the wall, fixing the panels firmly and neatly to the floor. But of course it *wasn't* attached to the half panel—that was the door to the hiding space. It had to be free to move. And so someone with an eagle eye just might notice that there was a slight gap between the smaller panel and the molding.

"Hey!" Sky said, hoping to distract the agent. "We just washed all those blankets." She made a show of brushing them off and piling them up neatly on the counter.

"Sorry," he said. He lifted the last blanket, saw nothing beneath it but the bottom of the chest, and didn't bother to remove it. "You can put them back now if you want."

Sky worked quickly, tossing the blankets into the box, two or three at a time. Then, shutting the lid, she slid the chest firmly back against the wall.

The agent hadn't moved. He was standing in the middle of the room, rubbing his chin, studying the space around him with squinty eyes. It was as if he sensed there was something about the room that wasn't quite right.

And there was, of course. It wasn't square anymore. It was one and a half panels deep but only one and a quarter panels wide. A foot and a half too narrow.

Worse, he seemed especially interested in that one particular wall. His eyes kept shifting back and forth across it. Finally he went over to the far corner and started knocking on the panels, all along the wall. He leaned his head forward, at an angle, listening for the regularly spaced *clunk* of the beams and the hollow *thunk* of the spaces between them.

He was nearing the spot where Kareem would be standing. It would sound different when he knocked there—not as hollow. Sky coughed loudly several times.

"Shhhh," the agent said. But he had passed the danger spot by then and kept on going—*Thuhk, thuhk, thunk, clunk! Thunk, thunk, thunk, clunk!*—all the way to the other end. He stepped back, unconsciously massaging the knuckles of his right hand.

Sky took a deep breath and let it out slowly. It was going to be all right, she told herself. It was going to be all right.

But now the agent went over to the blanket box again, slid it into the middle of the room, then leaned over and looked where the molding met the wall.

Sky was afraid she was going to puke. She'd just thought of yet *another* flaw in their wonderful hiding place. The panel was secured by a single latch, three feet off the ground. One good kick at floor level and it would bounce in, a quarter of an inch at least. Enough to make him really suspicious.

The agent nudged the panel with the toe of his shoe. He must have felt it give a little because now he adjusted his stance—bending his left knee and bringing his right foot back.

Sky's mind raced helplessly in circles. What should she do? What should she do? *What should she do?*

Then, *bam!* The agent let loose with a mighty kick—and the panel didn't budge.

It *didn't budge!*

She was slack-jawed at the wonder of it. Kareem, after that first tentative probe, must have known what was coming next. He'd had time to move his foot there, set it firmly against the panel. And it had worked. A genuine, certified miracle!

"What are you staring at?" the agent snapped. Judging by the pained look on his face, his toes would be sore for a week.

"I was just wondering, you know, why . . ." She made a kicking motion.

He shook his head and left the room. Sky slid the blanket box back in place for—what was it now, the third time? Fourth? She listened as the agent wandered pointlessly around the barn—in the stalls, up and down the breezeway. Finally he left.

But Sky stayed on, needlessly tidying the feed room, singing as she worked so Kareem would know she was there. Because she was so relieved, she chose her special song, the one she and Ana always used to sing together when Sky was a little girl. Back then, she'd believed her mother had written it especially for her. It had her name in it, after all.

The song had a lovely melody, and a swaying rhythm, and was chock-full of wonderful nonsense. It started out high and loud, then came down in stair-steps, becoming gradually lower and softer. They always exaggerated it, hitting that first "Ay!" really hard. And when they came to the last one, they'd always laugh.

"*Ay, ay, ay, ay,*" Sky sang. "*Canta y no llores.*"

She wondered if Kareem understood the Spanish. She hoped so. The words seemed right for the occasion: *Sing and don't cry.*

"*Porque cantando se alegran*"—Because singing makes you happy.

And then her favorite part: *Cielito lindo*—Pretty little Sky.

24

Farolitos

IT WAS WARM INSIDE, AND the house was filled with good cooking smells. Luke was in the kitchen, cutting up apples and onions to roast along with the chicken. Ana and the girls were gathered at the table, making *farolitos*. Muddy napped by the fire.

Sky treasured moments like this: everyone together, feeling cozy, working at happy tasks.

But it was all just a pretense. She felt neither happy nor cozy. And they most definitely were not all together. Kareem was still out in the feed room, alone and frightened. He'd been standing there, unable to move, in a space that felt like a grave, for almost three hours now. And there was no way of telling how much longer the agents would stay. They'd already searched the house, and the barn, and the *casita*, and the greenhouse, and the toolshed. What was left? The pump house? The chicken coop? Or were they out there stalking the property, peering behind chamisas and under piñons, craning their necks to check the highest branches of the apple trees?

How *did* you search sixty acres anyway? They could be there all night.

Sky had always loved the winter solstice. She looked forward to it every year—and not only because of the feast and the *farolitos*. Solstice was all about hope, and hope was a precious commodity just then. And so that morning when she'd awakened to the first snowfall of the season, long overdue and so incredibly beautiful, she'd declared it was going to be a perfect day. And it had been, right up to those last few seconds of the sled ride as they sped down the drive toward the gate. Until that moment, every single bit of it had been positively blissful!

Then the agents came and spoiled it, knocking all the happiness and hope right out of her.

The three of them worked in silence, Ana opening a paper bag, mechanically folding down the top a couple of inches to make it sturdier, then passing the bag on to Mouse, who filled it with sand—two cups each, carefully measured—and finally on to Sky, who put a candle in it and set it on a tray with all the others.

It was chilling, somehow, to perform this festive ritual so joylessly.

Sky heard the sound of footsteps on the *portal*. Then a couple of quick knocks and the door opened, bringing in a blast of frigid air. It wasn't the agent with the mustache. It was the other one, with the shaved head.

"I need the keys to your vehicles, please," he said.

Luke wiped his hands on a dishcloth. He looked, Sky thought, a good ten years older. Greenish, haggard. "I'll come with you," he said.

Ana got up and went over to her purse, took out her keys, and handed them to Luke.

Then they left, and she sat back down at the table and picked up another bag. They worked and waited.

By the time the men returned, maybe twenty minutes later, it was almost dark and the *farolitos* were finished. Sky had moved the trays to the coffee table, put the extra candles away, and set the bucket of sand in the corner by the stove. Now she was setting the table—for only four people, of course—while her mom put the finishing touches on their special solstice dinner.

The men came in together, Luke and both of the agents. Wordlessly, Luke put the keys to the Toyota back in Ana's purse.

"All right," Other Man said. "We're finished. Thank you for your cooperation."

Ana nodded.

"I hope you understand. This is no fun for us either.

We're just doing our jobs, trying to keep you safe."

Luke turned his head away. Sky thought any minute he was going to lose it. "I need to go with you," he said. "To let you out and lock the gate after you drive through."

Sky went on putting silverware down, hoping they wouldn't notice that her hands were shaking.

"All right," Mustache Man said. "Good night, ma'am."

They heard the motor start, then the crunch of tires in the snow.

Sky looked up at her mom. She was desperate to run to the feed room, right that minute, and let Kareem out. Bring him in where it was warm and make sure he was okay. Ana made a subtle gesture with her hand and shook her head. *Don't.*

Even now, Sky thought, with the agents driving away, they were afraid to speak out loud in their own house. She finished setting the table.

Luke would probably ride to the gate in the agents' van. Then he'd have to unlock it, let them through, lock up again, and walk all the way back. Seven minutes, maybe.

Sky kept checking her watch. It was taking too long. Ten minutes already.

And then the door opened and Kareem walked in.

25

A Light in the Darkness

HE WAS DIFFERENT. SKY NOTICED it right away.

He didn't respond normally, even when they asked him questions. He just went over to the stove and knelt there, still in his hat and parka, trembling with cold. His face was ashen. He looked haunted.

Sky sat down beside him, but he didn't acknowledge her. He just gazed hungrily into the fire.

Mouse came over and hovered, too. She watched him curiously for a bit, then looked at her sister with knitted brows. Sky shrugged. She didn't know what to think, or what to do.

Finally Mouse just asked, "Are you okay, Kareem?"

It was like he hadn't heard her.

"*Kareem?*" Mouse leaned over and gave him a close-up stare. He recoiled. "Are you *all right*?"

They were always asking him that, Sky thought. *Are you all right? Are you okay?* It must drive him crazy. "Leave him alone, Mouse."

"No," she said. "He doesn't look good."

"Hush."

But he was out of his daze now. He turned and looked at Mouse.

"Sorry." His voice was odd. "I was just . . . really . . . scared."

"Of course you were," Sky said. "We were *all* scared. You can't possibly be embarrassed about that!"

"No," he said. He spoke so softly she could scarcely hear him. "I just . . . it's taking me a while to feel safe again."

"I know."

"When he knocked on the wall . . ."

"That was awful! And then when he kicked the panel and you moved your . . ."

"Yeah."

Sky desperately wanted to hug him. That's what her family always did when one of them was frightened or sad—they hugged. But she was afraid he'd think it was weird.

"It helped when you were in there," he said. "Thanks for the song."

"Kind of silly, I know. I'm glad you liked it."

"But then after you left, I remembered about the

paintings, and I *knew* they'd be back, and they'd find me for sure." He gave a little shudder, just thinking of it.

"The paintings?" She was confused. Then, with a rush of horror, she remembered. They were right there in the *casita*, leaning against the wall—pictures of people with brown skin and dark hair, clearly done by a young artist.

"I kept thinking they'd come back any minute. . . ." He gasped out a lung full of air. "How could they have missed them?"

Ana came over, and knelt beside Kareem, and gave him the hug he needed.

"They just did," she said. "Some good spirit must have been watching over us. And now it's done. They've searched the whole place, and they didn't find you. There's no earthly reason for them to come back. So let's put it away now. They've robbed us of enough joy already. Let's don't give them any more."

When dinner was over, Luke and Ana carried the trays of *farolitos* outside and shut the door behind them.

"Put your parka back on," Sky told Kareem. "Hat and gloves, too. Trust me. This is something happy. You'll like it."

Mouse skipped over to the peg and got the parka for him. Her face was alight. She could never stay sad for long. "You need a scarf, too," she said. "Pick a color."

"I don't care. You choose."

She took her assignment seriously, digging through the basket of scarves, and gloves, and hats, rejecting a dark green muffler, then a maroon one. Finally she settled on golden yellow, the color of California poppies. When she handed it to Kareem, he actually smiled.

The door opened and Ana peeked in. "We're ready," she said. "Come on out."

The moon had not yet risen, and they'd turned off the lights in the house. It was incredibly dark outside. They had to feel their way down the *portal* steps.

"Stand over here," Luke said, guiding them one by one. "Close your eyes."

"Be patient," Sky whispered to Kareem. "This takes a while."

Match after match was struck. *Scrape, hiss. Scrape, hiss.* Finally the sounds stopped.

"All right," Luke said, "you can open them now."

"Ahhh," Sky said. It never ceased to thrill her, no matter how many times she'd seen them. All along the walkway, like twinkling fairy lights, flickering candles glowed through brown paper, casting a warm golden light out onto the snow.

"Oh!" Kareem said. "Wow." Sky smiled to herself. He liked them.

"They're called *farolitos*," Ana said. "'Little lamps.'"

Luke cleared his throat. "This is the longest night of the year," he began. "A turning point. From this moment on, the days will grow longer and the sun will be higher in the sky. Light will begin to drive out the darkness."

"At this time, more than ever," Ana continued, "we are suffering in the darkness and longing for the light. And so we especially welcome this new beginning."

"We will try to have hope," Sky said, "because we know there are seasons of light and seasons of darkness, but the sun always comes back to us."

"And even on the longest night of the year," Mouse said, "when it's really, really cold, we can still have things to cheer us up. Like the snow, and the *farolitos*, and riding on the sled."

Sky touched Kareem's arm. "You want to say something?" she whispered.

He shook his head.

"You sure?"

He nodded.

They waited a little while in case he changed his mind, then Luke brought the ceremony to a close.

"Even on the longest night of the year we can strike a match, and light a candle, and drive the darkness away. Even in the hardest times, when we think we may never be happy again, we discover that we can. We have each other, our friends, and our family. We have beauty, and kindness, and courage, and fun. And now that we have reached the darkest hour, we know the light is coming soon."

Sky looked over at Kareem; and in the glow of the little lanterns, she saw tears sparkling on his cheeks. She reached for his hand and gave it a squeeze.

"Happy solstice," she said softly.

He turned and looked at her; he didn't try to wipe away the tears.

"Happy solstice," he said.

26

The Secret

IT WAS THEIR FIRST DAY back after Christmas break.

Sky's group sat at a different table in the library now, over by the bank of windows. It was a little warmer there, and had more light. But the room was still cold, and the mood was glum.

Stef was in a rotten mood. She had nothing but complaints to offer. Her house was freezing. They hadn't been able to get much wood to burn in the fireplace; and even then, you practically had to sit on the hearth to get any warmth from it at all. They hadn't gone anywhere for the entire vacation (not that there was anywhere to go: no movies, no shopping, no nothing). They hadn't even had a Christmas tree; and there were hardly any presents, just the few things her mom had already bought before everything fell apart.

Oh, and their food really sucked.

"Cut it out, Stef," Graciela said. "It's the same for everybody."

"I bet *you* had a tree," Stef said to Sky, ignoring Graciela. "I bet you just went out and cut one."

"We don't do Christmas trees," Sky said.

"Oh, right. You pray to the moon or something."

Graciela stood up, gathered her things together, and moved to another table. Stef kept right on going.

"I bet you have lights out there. Right? All solar powered and everything?"

"Yes."

"And heat."

"We have a wood-burning stove."

"That works."

"Yes, it works."

"And hot water, too, I bet."

Sky heaved an exasperated sigh.

"You do, don't you?"

"Yes, Stef. We have hot water. Feel free to come out and take a shower anytime."

This was not feeling good to her at all. "I have to use the restroom," she said.

When she came back, everyone was getting up to leave. Mrs. Simmons must have called "time." The bell no longer rang.

Sky waited till Stef had gone, then followed the crowd down the breezeway toward the main building.

Suddenly she stopped and ducked behind a post. She'd caught sight of Gerald, surrounded by a bunch of boys. There seemed to be a lot of giggling; he looked ready to punch someone.

Sky wasn't going anywhere near *that*. She'd give him five minutes. Surely he'd have gone to class by then.

"You hiding from someone?" It was Mrs. Chavez.

"No," Sky said without thinking.

"Really?"

"Well, actually—Gerald."

"Ah." She was clearly amused. "Well, he seems to be gone now. And we'd better make it snappy or we're going to be late."

They continued together down the breezeway, now almost clear of students. It felt weird walking with a teacher like that, as though they were friends or something. She couldn't think of anything to say.

"I've been meaning to tell you," Mrs. Chavez said. "That was a wonderful essay you wrote."

"Oh, thanks. I was just lucky, I guess, that I hadn't planned to do PowerPoint or anything. That was kind of a problem for everybody else. With the electricity out and all."

"It's an *essay* contest, Sky. It always has been. Pictures, and music, and animation and all—they're fun, I know. But mostly they're just window dressing. The essays are meant to stand on their own. And yours had all the flash and dazzle built right in."

They'd reached Mrs. Chavez's classroom now, but the teacher stopped before going in and touched Sky's shoulder with a gentle hand.

"I've never had an essay before that was so . . . heartfelt."

Sky flushed with pleasure. "I was afraid it might be, like, too *critical.*"

"No, it was thoughtful and incredibly honest. And what you said about your feelings for your country—*despite* its problems and imperfections—that's what real love is all about, you know. Not fanatical devotion. I'm very proud of you, young lady. I asked you to think, and that's exactly what you did."

She gave Sky's shoulder a squeeze, then went into the classroom.

Sky continued down the hallway, trying to remember what the teacher had said, word for word, so she could repeat it to her parents later.

She saw Travis and Javier over by the water fountain. They were laughing, too. What was so hilarious all of a sudden? It made her a little uneasy. Could it—

She felt a hand on her arm, gripping her like a vise.

"Ow!" she said, turning around.

Gerald's trademark smirk was gone. He just looked angry now. "You're going to be *so* sorry," he said.

A group of girls passed them and giggled. Sky heard "hamster" and "pooped his pants," and Gerald squeezed even harder. She'd have a bruise there, no question.

"It wasn't me," she said. "I swear I didn't say a word!"

"Oh, sure."

"Honest! Cross my heart! Travis *begged* me to tell, and I told him to go away."

"Yeah, and yet somehow he knows all about it. I wonder how that happened."

"It had to be somebody else. There are at least six kids here who went to Alta Vista. It could have been any of them."

"They weren't in our class, Sky."

Actually, she realized, one of them was. Clayton Bracewell, a smart kid, a bit of a nerd, an occasional victim of Gerald's hilarity. Travis, so determined to learn the secret, must have spent *days* asking around (*"Did any of you go to Alta Vista?"*) until sooner or later he'd come to Clayton. *He* had no particular reason to keep Gerald's secret. After all, when the class bully opens up the hamsters' cage and stupidly expects the little critters to wait there patiently while he picks them up and stuffs them into the teacher's desk drawer, only instead they dash away like a bunch of escaped convicts, and then one of them happens to run up Gerald's pant leg and causes him to scream and let loose with the waterworks *and* the brown stuff, both simultaneously—well, that's the sort of story that's really fun to share. Especially if somebody asks.

For a split second Sky thought of bringing up Clayton's name. But she knew it wouldn't help. Gerald had nothing to lose now. Everybody already knew. All he had left was Sky's secret, and the prospect of revenge.

"Gerald, please!" She was more than willing to grovel if that would do any good. "It wasn't me. It wasn't! I'd be *crazy* to tell. Let go of my arm."

He shoved her up against the lockers and got right in her face. He was more than just angry, Sky realized. He was on the verge of tears. Gerald the bully was ruined. He would never get over this. She almost felt sorry for him.

"*Think* about it!" she pleaded. "*Why* would I tell? What's in it for me?"

"You'll find out," he said, giving her a shake and finally letting her go.

"No, Gerald! Please!" she called after him.

But it was too late. He was already gone.

27

A Quick Little Sunset Ride

THEY'D PLANNED TO GO OUT on a sunset ride that very same afternoon. It would be Kareem's first trail ride, and his first time off the Brightmans' property in almost three months. Everyone was really looking forward to it.

The route they would take—the only one that was safe for Kareem, and also by far the nicest—was known in the family as "the back way." It was accessed through the back gate, as the name implies; but it didn't lead to any road, just a narrow trail they had blazed themselves into the remotest part of the beautiful, unspoiled Pecos Wilderness. It was parkland, mountainous and green, with towering ponderosa pines and meadows with creeks running through them. There were ancient pueblo ruins out there, and the remains of an old adobe church, and petroglyphs, and any number of their own special, secret places.

Sky couldn't wait to share it with Kareem.

Only now it was totally spoiled. She couldn't think about sunsets and beautiful places. Her mind was stuck on Gerald, and what he'd threatened to do.

Nobody else blamed her for it. Not her mom, or her dad—not even Kareem. It meant they'd have to be even more careful now, since the agents would surely be back. Luke would make some minor adjustments to the false wall in the feed room. And they'd put Kareem's paintings in there, too, just to be on the safe side. It would be all right. The hiding place had worked before, and it would work again.

But Sky was in a deep blue mood, and she refused to be forgiven. She'd made such a holy muddle of things, starting with the blackmail, which was stupid, stupid, *stupid*! She'd needlessly dredged up a humiliating episode in the life of a notorious bully, knowing perfectly well what he was capable of. And though it *looked like* she'd done it to save Kareem from Gerald, she knew that wasn't the whole story. She'd also been trying to save herself, to wipe her slate clean of guilt and shame over her failure that day at Home Depot.

Oh, she was such an *unbelievable failure* at *everything*! Either she stood timidly by while injustice was done, or she acted on these harebrained, impulsive notions that only made things—

"*Sky!*" Ana said. "This isn't helping. Get over it! And . . ." She checked her watch. ". . . if you're going on that ride, you'd better hop to it."

Strange, the power Ana had to knock nonsense out of your head. It had long been a source of wonder to Sky, and she was deeply grateful for it now.

"Okay," she said, wiping her tears. "Let's do it."

The weather had been crisp and clear all day. But by the time they got the horses saddled, steel-gray clouds were beginning to gather behind the northwest mountains.

"You'd better keep an eye on that," Luke said. "Come back early if it starts to snow."

"We will."

"You refilled your saddle packs, Sky?"

"Yes, Daddy. Always."

"I'll go on ahead to open the gate," Mouse said. Luke was still adjusting Kareem's stirrups, and she was tired of waiting.

"Okay," Sky said. "We'll be along in a minute."

Mouse gave Peanut a little kick, and they trotted off.

"Stand up in the stirrups, Kareem," Luke said. "Let me have a look-see."

Kareem rose a few inches out of the saddle.

"How's it feel?"

"Fine."

"If they're too short, your knees will hurt."

"I know. They're all right."

"Then I guess you're good to go. Take it easy, Sky. All right? It's Kareem's first time out."

"I will, Daddy."

"That's what you always say."

"This time I mean it."

"And keep an eye on—"

"The weather. Got it."

They were just leaving the barn, with Mouse well out of sight, maybe already at the gate, when they heard the sound of a motor coming at them very fast. They turned and stared, dumbstruck, as a silver van came speeding around the curve and up the drive.

"I don't believe it," Luke said, aghast. "They *cut our fence!*"

In the Old West, that was a hanging offense. It still amounted to breaking and entering. Luke sprinted back to the house, beside himself with rage.

"Go! Go!" Sky called to Kareem.

He nudged Blanca with his heels and she began to walk, though not very fast.

"*Harder!*"

Blanca shifted to a fast walk.

The agent with the ginger mustache jumped out of the van and thundered up the steps to the *portal*.

"Get off my property this minute!" Luke shouted,

running up to him. "I'm calling the police. You have absolutely *no right*—"

Ana heard the commotion and opened the door. Muddy ran out and stood on the *portal*, barking excitedly.

"Where is he?" Mustache Man said.

"Who?"

"Over there!" the other agent shouted. He had just spotted Kareem riding away from the barn.

"Kick her!" Sky screamed. *"Hard!"*

Kareem did, and Blanca bolted forward so suddenly that he almost lost his seat.

"Go after him!" the agent called, tossing the keys to his partner.

But Muddy, bless his ancient soul, got there first. He flew off the porch, jaws wide, and made a perfect catch in mid-air. He was so proud of this feat, he decided to take a victory lap, running around and around in circles, his prize in his mouth.

Luke stopped in his tracks and burst out laughing.

Kareem turned in the saddle to see what was going on. Blanca read this as a signal to stop.

"Go!" Sky yelled. "Follow Mouse's tracks!"

He nudged Blanca again, just hard enough this time, and off they went.

Sky waited near the barn. She had some vague plans of distracting the agents, giving Kareem a little more time to get away. Also, it was awfully entertaining to watch a pair of muscle-bound agents, in their suits and ties and shiny lace-up shoes, chasing an elderly dog around a slushy yard, shouting like maniacs.

It took them almost a minute, but the agents finally cornered Muddy and retrieved their keys. Then they piled back into the van and started the motor.

Only then, apparently, did they realize they didn't know which way to go. Kareem was out of sight; and with snow all over everything, it was even hard to tell what was a road and what was not.

Sky took off, and as she'd hoped, the van came speeding after her, bouncing and sliding on the uneven terrain. Perfect, Sky thought as she led them around the barn, then back toward the *casita* and on past the big cluster of junipers to the left.

She hadn't planned what happened next, though later it seemed like genius.

When the sky is overcast, the light on snow becomes "flat." You can't see dips or bumps in the ground till you're practically on them. It's something skiers know. Sky knew it, too—only she'd been distracted, and she was excited, and she'd forgotten what lay straight ahead of her. By the time she remembered, it was too late to turn.

But Prince had been a jumper in his younger days. Though he'd long since been demoted to trail horse, he still knew what to do. With the grace of a champion, he sailed over that snowy mound. Seconds later, the van plowed into it.

The manure pile.

28

Pretend You're a Shepherd

"Do you know where we're going?" Karem asked. The trail had left the rolling landscape a good half hour before. Now it had narrowed and was rising steadily, skirting the edge of a steep hill, a cliff to their left, a drop off to their right.

"Five more minutes," Sky said.

The weather had turned very quickly. The wind was kicking up now, and clouds covered the sky, dark and low. So far there were only a few flakes, but that was probably just the beginning. They needed to get to shelter soon.

The trail widened again, and around the bend Sky spotted their destination—Petroglyph Cave.

It wasn't really a cave, just a massive slab of hard rock, and below it a deep layer of softer rock that had worn away over the centuries, forming a shallow, room-sized shelter.

Carved along the front edge of the overhanging slab was a single, enormous petroglyph. Time had weathered it. In places you could barely see that anything was there. But the raking light and clinging snow picked up the subtle indentations, patiently chipped out ages ago by some ancient cliff dweller: a snake, its body rising and falling in zigzag fashion, its head sprouting two tiny horns.

The horned water serpent. A god of the Pueblo people, Luke had told them. He wasn't too sure about the details.

"It's our special place," Mouse said.

"Did you build that?" Kareem was pointing to a crude coyote fence—upright sticks lashed together with wire—that curved around the near side of the shelter. It looked like something two kids might have made. It leaned to the side, and it wasn't very tidy.

"Yeah," Sky said. "It's kind of raggedy looking, I know. But it blocks the wind and keeps the snow from blowing in."

They dismounted, and led the horses in under the overhang, and tied them to a makeshift hitching post: a stout stick supported by a mound of rocks. The horses shifted to stand facing the wind.

"Shepherds used to sleep up here," Sky said. "Back in the olden days. We found the ruins of an old fence, so we built ours in the same place. Hey, Kareem, can you hand me that saddle pack? Actually, why don't you bring them all?"

He dropped them on the floor of the cave. Sky squatted down, opened one of the packs, and started pulling things out: a leather work glove, a box of matches, and a small flashlight. "Here, Mouse, hold this."

There was a large stack of wood in the corner. Sky put on the glove, kicked the woodpile a couple of times, then, with Mouse beside her holding the flashlight, started picking up logs.

"Why did you do that?" Kareem asked.

"Black widow spiders."

"Ew."

"Yeah. They like to hang out in woodpiles. It probably doesn't do any good; I'm just kind of giving 'em fair warning. The glove's really the important thing. That, and having enough light to see them by."

She carried the logs over and dropped them beside the circle of stones. Then she proceeded to build her fire, starting with the kindling: a heap of broken twigs and dried pine needles. Around them she erected a tepee of logs. When she was satisfied with the arrangement, she struck a match and set the wood alight.

Carefully, methodically, she tended the flame. In a few minutes she had a roaring fire. The wood was bone-dry.

The three of them huddled together, enjoying the warmth—Mouse in the middle because she was shivering.

"We've got enough wood to last us for days," Sky said.

"And all that stuff in the saddle packs—water, and power bars, and trail mix, and dried fruit."

No food for the horses, though, she thought but didn't say.

"Is that the plan, then? To stay out here for days?"

"Well, Kareem, if you'll remember, we don't actually *have* a plan. I mean, we weren't expecting . . . I guess we just wait and see what happens."

"See if the agents come after us or not?"

"No. I don't think they can. They'd need horses, or maybe an ATV, to get here. And anyway, they don't know where we are, and it's getting dark, and the trail's not marked. With this wind and snow, they wouldn't even be able to follow our tracks."

"So—what exactly are we waiting for?"

"Dad'll come out and get us when it's safe to come home."

"Don't you have a phone? Can't he just call?"

"No reception out here."

"Oh. Does he know where we are?"

"He'll figure it out. It's our favorite place; and we have shelter here, and plenty of wood. He helped us gather it in August. It's the logical place for us to go in a snowstorm."

"And how is he going to get out here? We have all the horses."

"I don't know, Kareem. Borrow one from a neighbor, I guess."

"I don't want to spend the night here," Mouse whimpered.

"We've been out in worse than this."

"Not all night."

"Just pretend you're a shepherd."

They sat for a while in silence, staring dumbly at the dancing flames. The warmth on their faces was beginning to make them languid and dreamy. Sky shut her eyes. There was something deeply primal about sitting by a fire, warm, while all about you the tempests roared. It put her in touch with her inner cavewoman. She imagined herself, hairy and ape-like, crouching before the mysterious flames, surrounded by her family of hairy, ape-like . . .

"What time is it?" Mouse asked.

Sky pushed up the sleeve of her parka and looked at her watch.

"Almost seven."

"It feels later than that. I'm hungry."

"Want some fruit?"

"Yeah."

Sky fished a sandwich bag from one of the packs. It was filled with pale crescents: little slices of dried apple. Mouse began nibbling them, mouse-like, tiny bits at a time.

The wind was coming in at a different angle now. It blew into the far corner of the cave, producing an unsettling wail. *Whooo, whooooooooo.* It made the horses nervous.

"That sounds like a ghost," Mouse said, making an anxious face.

"It is," Sky told her solemnly. "It's the ghost of an Indian who used to live here. He's saying *whooooo* is that little girl eating apples in my cave? *Whoooooooooooo!*"

"Quit it, Sky! You're scaring me!"

"I'm sorry, baby. Come here." She opened her arms, and Mouse scrambled over for a hug. Then gradually Mouse slipped down till she was lying on the ground, her head in Sky's lap. She seemed comfortable there.

The coyote fence was leaning more than it had when they first arrived. The wind was blowing hard against it, and the snow was weighing it down. Someday—maybe soon, maybe even tonight—the whole thing would collapse. They'd need Luke's help to put it back up again.

The wailing grew louder. Even Sky found it disturbing now. It really *did* sound like a ghost, and the ghost seemed to be speaking to her. Warning her. Rebuking her. Asking her *what the heck she thought she was doing*, dragging everybody out here on a night like this.

She looked over at Kareem. He hadn't said anything in quite some time. He just sat there, staring at the fire, his expression strangely flat. He was thinking the whole situation over, Sky knew, counting all the reasons why this wasn't going to work, why staying out there was stupid and dangerous.

She tried to shut that thought out of her mind. What, after all, was the alternative? Going back and surrendering to the agents? No. They just needed to be creative, that was all. And a little more help from those good spirits definitely wouldn't hurt.

Sky closed her eyes again and began:

O, spirits of the cave—whoever you are, whoever you were in life—I call on you now to help this boy. He is innocent, and he is in danger. Give him the strength and the courage he needs. Drive away the storm; bring out the stars and the moon. Keep us safe, here in your cave, for just a little while. If you are powerful, and you are still here, I beg you to help us now.

29

Saving Sky

"Sky?"

"What?"

They spoke in low voices. Mouse had fallen asleep.

"This doesn't make any sense."

She winced; she'd known this was coming. "We're waiting till it's safe to go back home," she said.

"What does that *mean*? Safe how?"

"Safe from the agents. When they leave . . ."

"But they're not *going* to leave."

"Of course they are. They're not planning to move in with us."

"Come on, Sky. They *saw* me. They know I've been staying at your house, and they know where I am. Or at least the important part: that we're somewhere out in the Pecos Wilderness—three kids, alone at night, in a snowstorm."

"So?" She was *not* giving in to this poisonous logic.

"It isn't a real escape. It never was. They know sooner or later we're going to come home. And if we don't, your parents will get so freaked out worrying about us, they'll figure out a way to bring us back themselves. The agents aren't leaving, Sky. They'll still be there in the morning."

"Then we'll just have to wait them out."

She stirred the coals and added another log.

"We have to go back," he said.

She turned and glared at him. "No! They'll arrest you!"

"Of course they will. Don't you *get* it? We could stay out here a *week*, and starve, and freeze—and they'd *still* arrest me. It's over. I can't live in your house anymore."

"But—"

"I have to turn myself in."

"No, Kareem—wait! I have an idea. It's a good one. We have food, and water, and shelter, and a fire. The snow is bound to let up soon."

"Why? What makes you say that?"

"Just listen. Tomorrow we'll ride over to one of the pueblos. Tesuque's the closest. They'll take you in, Kareem; I know they will. And tribal lands are sovereign territory. I don't think the agents can even go in there, not without permission."

"Oh, good, let me get this straight. We're going to ride

over to the Tesuque Pueblo—like two days' trekking in the snow, assuming we can even find it—then we'll knock on some random stranger's door and ask if I can live with them? That's crazy. You just made that up on the spot."

"No, I didn't."

"Yeah, you did."

A huge gust of wind shook the coyote fence again; snow blew into their faces and into the fire.

"We can't stay out here all night."

"Shepherds did it."

"No, Sky. Shepherds go out in the *summertime*, when there's grass and stuff for the sheep to eat. Not in January. And anyway, it doesn't matter what the shepherds did. We have to go back. This storm is just going to get worse."

"It'll be better in the morning. I just have this feeling."

"Maybe. Or maybe we'll all die of hypothermia."

"Oh, that's stupid, Kareem. We have down parkas on, and gloves, and hats, and boots. Mountain climbers—"

"Oh, stop it! I don't give a flip about shepherds and mountain climbers. It's freezing out here, even with the windbreak and the fire. And it's not safe. If you don't care about yourself, then think about Mouse."

"You *want* to go back? Is that it? You want to ride away with those agents in their silver van so they can lock you up in that deportation center for—"

"Of *course* not."

"All right, then—"

"But I don't have a *choice*. See, that's the difference between you and me: I don't walk around with this la-la fantasy that everybody's story has a happy ending. Sometimes life just—"

"—sucks. Yeah, I got that part. And I know they probably *will* get you in the end, and we'll have spent a really miserable time out here for nothing; but I just can't *stand* the thought of your going back there and turning yourself in!"

"Look, Sky, you can't fix this," he said. "I know you want to—you'd like to save the whole world if you could. But this is *way* over your head. Please, *please*, just give me the . . . dignity . . . of going back there and dealing with my own problem by myself."

She closed her eyes. She wasn't sure she'd ever felt so hopeless in her life.

"Sky?"

"What?" She was crying now, not caring that she was making a fool of herself.

"Those terrible things I said. I didn't mean them. Really."

"What terrible things?"

"You know. Like you're weird, and crazy, and live in a time warp. I hurt your feelings when you were trying to be nice. I hate that I said that. I was just crazy-angry, and scared; and I took it out on you."

177

"I know that. I knew it all along."

"But you didn't deserve to be treated—"

"Apology accepted, Kareem. Let it go."

"I can't. Your family, and the way you've all looked after me, and risked yourselves for me—I can't believe there are people like you in the world. And you *don't* live in la-la land. You . . ." He was choking up now. "You made your own world out there in that beautiful place, and it's better than the real one, and I'm so grateful you let me live in it."

"You still can."

"You know that's not true. Mouse, wake up. We're leaving."

He got up and brushed the snow off his jacket.

Sky stayed where she was, looking up at him, feeling sick.

"Sky?" Mouse said, tugging at the sleeve of her parka.

"Don't go." Sky's voice was expressionless. She just had to say it one more time.

Kareem led Blanca outside and put his left foot into the stirrup, just as Sky had taught him, and pulled himself up, right leg swinging over the saddle, and sat for a bit, looking down at them.

"I sure hope I don't get lost on the way back," he said. "Or fall off your stupid horse. It would *really* help if I had somebody with me who knew the way home."

PART THREE

Four Months Later

30

The Winners

THE EVENING BEGAN WITH A five-minute speech by the superintendent of schools. He was followed by the mayor, who was followed by the senator. The governor would go last; she got to introduce the winners.

Sky gazed out into the dimly lit room. With its white plaster walls and high, high ceiling supported by elaborately painted wooden beams, it looked more like an old New Mexican church than any auditorium she'd ever seen. There was a wooden choir loft in the back, and along the side walls were arched *nichos* with some kind of religious frescoes in them—like stained-glass windows without the glass.

All the seats were filled. In the side aisles, TV cameras were rolling, while news-site photographers crept around up front, just below the stage. Every now and then, as someone new came up to the podium, a string of flashes would blast out of the darkness.

So many people! And in just a few minutes they'd all be staring at her.

There was huge applause as the governor got up to speak. She was famously short, so she reached around and slid the little step-box over, the one that was there for the children. The audience laughed as she suddenly gained six inches, and they clapped again.

She said pretty much the same thing all the others had: that these wonderful children were our state's future—indeed, our *nation's* future! They were a true inspiration, and they filled us with hope!

"I know it takes *courage*"—she turned to the three petrified children sitting behind her—"to stand up here and read your essays before such an enormous crowd." She paused, got her laugh, and went on. "And if anyone should ask me tonight *what I love about my country*, I'll tell them, it's children like you!"

Sky looked for what was surely the hundredth time at her family, right up front in their special reserved seats. They were all smiling. Luke was giving her a thumbs-up. She took a deep breath.

And then the governor introduced the third-place winner: Jacob Chu from Albuquerque. Jacob walked over to the podium, stepped up on the little platform, and announced the title of his essay: "America: A Mosaic."

He clicked the remote presenter, and the sound of a single violin filled the room. *O beautiful for spacious skies, for amber waves of grain.*

It was Jacob playing, of course. He had recorded himself.

Now a picture came up on the screen, a wilderness scene from a national park. As the music played softly in the background and snowcapped mountains were replaced by a river, then a waterfall, then a hot orange desert with dramatic cliffs, Jacob began to read his essay. The first part of the mosaic: *America is beautiful.*

Then the landscapes gave way to a market in Chinatown, followed by mariachis in full regalia, and a bunch of little Hasidic boys, with their side curls and yarmulkes, playing soccer in the street.

America is a land of many peoples.

Next came the Old North Church in Boston, and the Taos Pueblo, and the Alamo.

America has a rich and varied history.

And so it went. He'd built his essay from many small parts, each a facet of American life, or its landscape, or its culture, or its arts, or its history. Eventually, as with a mosaic or a puzzle, all those little parts—the words, the music, and the pictures—came together to form a whole: a rich and complex image of the country he loved.

The last slide was a computer-generated mosaic made from all the previous pictures. They were arranged according to their dark or light values to form an image of the Statue of Liberty.

America! America! God shed His grace on thee, And crown thy good with brotherhood from sea to shining sea!

Sky was flabbergasted. She'd never seen anything like it. And this kid won *third place?*

Once again the governor went to the podium, this time to introduce the second-place winner: Maria Perez from Farmington. Maria had chosen to write about courage, and her essay couldn't have been more different from the one they'd just heard.

She fiddled nervously with the remote, and after a few seconds a picture came up on the screen. It was a formal group portrait of her family, everyone dressed up and smiling at the camera. It was her one and only slide. As it turned out, she didn't need any others.

In the simplest language, Maria carried the audience step by step through each excruciating stage of a family's descent into crisis—the grandmother with diabetes, the baby brother with asthma, the father laid off from his job, the repossessed car, the struggle to come up with the rent on their little apartment—till she came to the decision by her older brother to drop out of high school and join the army to help pay the family's bills.

One of the brother's teachers had begged him not to go, to wait at least till he graduated. He was such a promising student, she'd said. He had a real future.

His mother had burst into tears and said they'd manage somehow. Please don't go.

But he went anyway.

He'd only been there a week when he was killed by a roadside bomb.

Yet there he still was, up on the screen, frozen in time: a stocky boy, his hair cut military-style, wearing his uniform proudly. The picture must have been taken right before he deployed.

The audience was fishing for Kleenex in pockets and purses, and sniffling, and wiping their eyes.

Maria's brother had been awarded a medal called a Purple Heart. It hung on the wall in the family's living room, framed under glass, so they could look at it every day and remember the sacrifice he'd made for his country, and for them.

But she wished he could have *seen* it, just once before he died, maybe even had his commanding officer pin it on his uniform at a ceremony, something like that. She hated that he never knew what a hero he'd been.

As Maria returned to her seat at the back of the stage, the audience jumped to their feet, and clapped, and cheered. A powerful wave of emotion was moving through the room.

It was extraordinary.

The governor stood, clapping along with the audience, till everyone finally sat down. Then, for the third time, she advanced to the podium.

It was Sky's turn now, and she didn't know how she could possibly follow something like that. But she *had* to, and she had to do it right. Everything depended on it.

She was trembling with fear. Mrs. Chavez, who sat beside her, reached over and squeezed her hand.

"Thank you, Maria," the governor said. She put her hand to her heart and sighed. "That was truly an inspiration."

There was more applause, and the governor waited respectfully. Then she allowed a few more beats of silence before giving the final introduction.

"Ladies and gentlemen, it is now my great pleasure to introduce to you the first-place winner of the State of New Mexico Land of Enchantment Essay Contest—*Sky Brightman of Pecos!*"

31

Her Best Blessing Yet

SKY LAID THE DARK BLUE folder on the podium, but she didn't open it yet. She took a deep breath, trying to get herself under control, then leaned toward the mike and said the first thing that popped into her head.

"Wow."

The audience laughed.

"When we . . . when our teacher, Mrs. Chavez, gave us this assignment, she was very specific about one thing. Well, actually, she was specific about quite a few things, but the one that comes to mind right now is when she said, and I quote, 'You're not going to win, so get that out of your heads right now.'"

The audience loved it. They were with her all the way.

Good, she thought, stay there, please.

"So"—she opened her folder—"I, um, chose to write

about 'What I Love About My Country.' And to be honest, I thought my essay was kind of weird—but I guess it was better than I thought."

She looked up, and forced her face into a smile, and they laughed again.

"Now, the reason I'm telling you all this is that I'm afraid you'll have to use your imaginations as to how good it actually was, because I didn't bring it here tonight."

There was a great intake of breaths, and some not-so-quiet murmuring.

"*But,*" she went on quickly, "there's something else I want to read, and I guarantee it's a whole lot better than my essay."

She held it up for them to see. She knew she had less than a minute to grab them before somebody got out the hook.

"Unfortunately, the person who wrote it couldn't turn it in because it wasn't safe for him to go to school. If he did, he'd be arrested."

By now the gasps and the murmuring were almost drowning her out.

"And I think that if you'll just *do me this favor,* just *give me a few minutes,* you'll understand why I'm doing this. *Please!*"

The room gradually grew quiet. Sky's heart was pounding. They were going with it. No one was stopping her.

"The author of this essay is a boy named Kareem Khalid. He's my friend, and he hid in our house for about three months. After he left, we found his notebook. Maybe I shouldn't have read it; but I did, and there was a lot of amazing stuff in there. He's a really good writer.

"I knew he'd done an essay on why he loved America even though he couldn't turn it in or anything. We talked about it. But it turns out he wrote the other one, too, the one on courage. That's what I want to read to you tonight."

Sky pressed the forward button on the remote presenter, and a painting came up on the screen: a middle-aged man with a crooked smile.

"All of the pictures were done by Kareem. He, well, he didn't have anything to remember his family by, so he painted them himself."

She cleared her throat and began to read.

What Is the Meaning of Courage?
By Kareem Khalid

Years ago, in a faraway place, there was a boy who loved rock music. He bought some tapes from a man in the street and went home and played them. But where he lived, that kind of music was illegal. A neighbor reported him to the authorities, and he was sent to prison. He was only fourteen.

The boy was there for six months. His parents brought food to the prison every day and bribed the guards to give it to him. But the guards ate it themselves, and all the boy ever got was prison food, so he grew thinner and thinner, weaker and weaker.

Still, he refused to give up hope. He wasn't going to be like so many other prisoners, the ones who just lay on the floor, broken and depressed, hardly saying a word. He decided he needed a project, something to take his mind off his fears. So he made up stories in his head about his cell mates. He tried to imagine what their old lives had been like, and what crimes had brought them there. He memorized those stories word for word because he wasn't allowed to have any writing materials. During the time the boy was in prison, some of those people died. But because he refused to let his jailors break his spirit, he survived.

That boy was my father, and he had courage.

Sky looked at the audience for the first time. There was absolute dead silence out there. She pressed the remote again, and the next slide came up: a head-and-shoulders painting of an older couple. The woman had short, wavy hair and large eyes. The man wore glasses, and his mustache was gray. Kareem had painted it from his imagination. He didn't actually know what they looked like.

When the boy got well again, his parents sent him and his older brother away to school in England. They had to sell their apartment to raise the money to pay the bribes, and they knew they might never see their sons again. But they wanted them to be free. They wanted them to be safe. While the boy was at the university, his parents were killed because of their beliefs.

They were my grandparents, and they had courage.

Sky advanced to the next slide. Another couple, well dressed and handsome, the man quite a bit older than the woman. This was also done from Kareem's imagination. He'd never seen a picture of them, either.

At the same time there was a girl growing up on the other side of the city. She loved books and was good with numbers, but she couldn't go to school because she was a girl. So her father, who was a doctor, taught her at home.

Then there was an epidemic of cholera, and the father caught it, and he died. As soon as the girl turned thirteen, her grandparents arranged a marriage for her. The man they picked was rich, but he was old and very strict. The girl was afraid of him, and didn't want to get married. She just sat in her room and cried and cried.

The girl's mother didn't know what to do. Her in-laws wouldn't listen to her, and she didn't have anything

of her own except some jewelry, and a silk rug, and her
clothes. She couldn't even leave the house alone. Women
were always supposed to have a proper male escort. But
she was determined to help her daughter. So she offered
to give the rug to a neighbor—an old man—if he would
drive her and her daughter to the mother's home village.
She told him she was going there to visit her family, and
he agreed.

The village was near the border. When they got there,
the mother gave most of her jewelry to a cousin; and in
exchange he escorted the girl across the border, and got her a
fake passport, and bought her a ticket to London, and made
sure she got on the plane.

Later, the mother was killed by the husband's family.
They said she had shamed them by what she had done.

That was my grandmother, and she had courage.

There were little gasps and hushed whispers coming
from the audience now. Sky clicked the remote again.

The next slide was Sky's favorite. It showed a girl with
long, black hair and dark, dramatic eyebrows. Her dress
was pink. She was very young, and very pretty. Out in the
auditorium, people went "Ahhh."

The girl had two of her mother's rings, and she sold
them for money to live on. But it wasn't enough, so she

scrubbed floors, and emptied trash in office buildings, and washed dishes in a Chinese restaurant. Later, they let her wait tables, and that's how she met the nice couple who offered to help her. They arranged with a lawyer to get her legal residence papers, and gave her a little room in their house to sleep in. It was actually just a closet, so it didn't have a window. It didn't have any furniture either, just a mattress on the floor. But it was warm, and it was safe. She was glad to have it.

The family let her go to school, but in her free time she cleaned their house and looked after their children. Late at night she did her homework. But she was smart, and she worked hard. When she graduated, she won a scholarship to the University of London.

That girl was my mother, and she had courage.

Now came a wedding picture. The bride wasn't wearing a long gown and a veil, just a pale blue dress. But she was carrying flowers, and the man had on a black suit. He wasn't much taller than she was. They looked very happy.

The girl met the boy in chemistry class. They liked to say that they had such good chemistry they fell in love instantly. Right after graduation they got married and went to the United States, where they spent a total of nine years studying to become doctors, and doing their internships and their residencies. Only then did they find out that patients didn't want to go to them because of their foreign name, and their accents, and especially because of the place where they were born, which was where many of the terrorists came from.

Then, during the flu pandemic, the wife got sick and died, and the husband was left with a son to raise and a terrible sadness in his heart. But he still refused to let hardship break his spirit. He spent another four years training in a new specialty—anesthesia—where patients wouldn't have to look at him so much. Even then, the only place that would hire him was a small community hospital in New Mexico. But he was glad to have a job, and to be a citizen of a free country, where he could work in peace, and believe as he wished, and give his son a good life.

Then one day some federal agents came to the hospital where he worked and put him under arrest, even though he hadn't done anything wrong.

The audience gasped. Sky looked out at the dark sea of faces and waited. Let them think about it, remember what this man had already been through, understand exactly what it meant. Then she found her place again, and went on.

He didn't know where the agents were taking him, or what would happen to him there. He must have been very frightened. But all he could think of was his son. And so, in secret, he asked a friend—a nurse who was standing nearby—to please take care of his boy. She agreed to do it. After that he left with dignity.

Those were my parents, and they had courage.

Sky clicked the remote again and there they were, her whole family. Luke, handsome and blond, towering over tiny Ana, so small and dark. Sky's arm was draped over Mouse's shoulder, and Mouse was patting Muddy, who looked very fat and old, and seemed to be smiling.

The agents went to the son's school because they wanted to arrest him, too, though he was only thirteen. But the nurse got to him first, and drove him out to her house, and hid him there. This was against the law, and it put her family in danger. But the nurse, and her husband, and her children welcomed him with their whole hearts, because they believed it was the right thing to do. And they risked themselves many times for the boy's sake, but they were glad to do it.

Those people are my friends, and they have courage.

Sky's voice broke when she came to that part. She had

to take a deep breath to get it under control. She glanced quickly out into the silent room, then brought up the last slide. It was Kareem's self-portrait. Luke had made a frame for it, and it hung in their living room—like the medal Maria's brother had earned—so they could look at him every day and say a blessing for him every night.

I don't know how it will end for my father, or the nurse and her family, or for me. But these stories have taught me a lot about courage.

I know that having courage doesn't mean you aren't afraid. It means that even when you are, especially when you are, you keep on doing what you have to, and what is right.

Courage doesn't have to be dramatic, like a firefighter running into a burning building to save a child. Sometimes it's a simple thing, like admitting you were wrong, or putting your needs aside for the good of others. Sometimes when things are hard in a person's life, it takes courage just to keep going.

I think back on the story of my family, and I know that I wouldn't be here, safe, and protected, and free, if it weren't for the courage of so many others. And I hope I can live up to that gift, and have courage myself, so that I can do for others what was done for me.

Sky put Kareem's essay back in the folder and closed it.

"The boy who wrote that essay isn't 'safe, and protected, and free.' Not anymore. He's in one of those deportation centers, here in New Mexico. His father—the man who was so proud to be a citizen of a free country—he's in there, too, along with lots and lots of other innocent people.

"In case you're wondering, my parents got in trouble for what they did. They were charged with conspiracy for hiding Kareem at our house. And they pleaded guilty because, well, they really *had* committed a crime. But the judge called it an "unjust law," an "*idiotic* law"—right there in court. Then she sentenced my parents to a year of community service, growing crops for the food bank, which we already do. We've been doing it for years.

"That judge had courage, too. She refused to punish good people for acting on their consciences. She said that would be *wrong*. And she said it out loud, in public.

"So I just have to ask you—everybody here in this room, and all of you who are watching us on TV—*don't you agree with her?* That it's *wrong?* What would happen if all of us acted like she did? If we stopped being afraid and just spoke the truth."

In the front row, Sky's parents, and Mouse, and Aunt Pat, and Ms. Golly were standing up now; and Sky felt a thrill run up her spine.

"It's not easy for one person to fight a thing like this. But we could all do it together. We could—I don't know—put signs in our yards and in shop windows. We could write letters to the president. We could have a rally on the plaza."

Out in the audience, several more people were getting to their feet. Sky felt tears stinging her eyes. She was trembling all over.

"And Mrs. Governor . . ."

"*Madame* Governor" came a whisper from behind her. Mrs. Chavez, of course.

"Sorry," Sky said. "*Madame* Governor, and all you other important people here, if you'll help us, we can change this. We don't have to let it happen in our state. And if we stop it here, maybe it'll stop in other places, too."

She heard a rustling behind her, and she turned. Mrs. Chavez was standing, and so were Maria, and Jacob, and their teachers. Then the rustling became a rumble as person after person, out there in the dark, stood up.

Sky rested her hands firmly on the podium, closed her eyes, and began gathering up everything good from within her spirit—warmth, love, kindness, strength, humor, honesty, righteousness, loyalty, courage. Behind her, the scraping of chairs said the dignitaries were standing now, too. But Sky kept her focus, letting the force of good things continue to build inside her till the heat of it burned in her chest. Then she let it go, and her blessing burst out into that beautiful room that looked like a church, and through the walls, and into the street, and across the plaza where the first buds of spring were breaking out, and on past the empty hotels, and the shops, and the few dimly lit restaurants, and through the hundreds of little neighborhoods, then on up into the hills, and out across the quiet countryside—spreading, growing, flowing endlessly across the varied landscapes of a great and beautiful country.

Her best blessing yet.

Acknowledgments

I WOULD LIKE TO THANK Tracy Reid and Kristin Taglienti for their guidance in the matter of horses; Molly Kelly, for reading yet another manuscript and giving me her usual wise advice; my husband, Peter, for listening to countless versions of this story for much too long, and killing off characters who needed to go, and giving me more wise advice; and finally, Rosemary Brosnan, my wonderful editor, who was endlessly patient, and thoughtful, and kind, and who gave me the key when I was stuck, because she's so good at what she does.